RUMOR HAS IT

RH TUCKER

EVERGOLD PRESS

Edited by DominionEditorial.com
Cover design by James at GoOnWrite.com

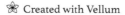 Created with Vellum

Chapter 1

Carter

"Shots!"

Jeremy yells out to everyone gathered around his patio. His parties have been hit and miss over the past four years.

Last year, he had an awesome after-prom party. Being juniors, he invited some seniors to keep up the 'cool' factor. Tonight's party isn't for any special occasion. His parents are out of town for the weekend, both of them realtors who specialize in commercial real estate. So, having a party in Quail Hill, a house that cost Jeremy's parents over three million dollars–something he loved to point out when they moved in right before our junior year–always impresses people.

I look over at Matt as we lounge in a hot tub, the sun setting over the backyard.

"Dude, I'm not doing shots." I laugh. "If he'd held this party yesterday like he said he was going to, then maybe.

But I'm not showing up at school tomorrow with a hangover."

Matt nods, looking over at Jeremy pouring the alcohol into shot glasses. I can tell he's thinking about it but then wraps his hands behind his head, leaning back in the hot tub. "True."

Matt's my best friend. I've known him since third grade, but we became good friends when we started high school at Woodbridge High. Jeremy is cool, but he can definitely rub people the wrong way. And sometimes, whatever he says is just plain stupid or dickish. Sometimes both. But we all play sports together and have been hanging out since the beginning of high school.

I lean back, enjoying the hot tub. Another great perk of Jeremy's parties. Summertime we could jump in the pool, but if it's cold, we hit the hot tub.

"Hey, you got Mr. Hilton's assignment from Friday, right?" Matt says

"What assignment?" I ask lazily, still enjoying the water.

We had an away game for basketball, so we left school early for the bus ride. Mr. Hilton is our calculus teacher and does not give any students slack on missing assignments. Not that our team deserved it. We weren't bringing any titles to Woodbridge High anytime soon.

"It was, like, five chapters I think. He said it was so much because it counts for double points on your grade."

My eyes pop open. "Shit. What's the assignment? I can't let my grade drop."

"Don't you have an A in the class?"

"Yeah, but my graduation trip, remember?"

My mom promised that if I aced every class my entire senior year, she'd get me a week's vacation to anywhere I wanted to go. We aren't rich by any means, so I know how big of a deal it is. The only real caveat is that I have to stay in the country. I've narrowed down my choices to Miami or New York.

"Oh, yeah."

I wait for him to say something else, but he closes his eyes, leaning lower into the hot tub. "Well?"

"Bro, I don't remember. He broke it up. I want to say chapters twenty-one to twenty-three. And then ... forty-five and forty-seven?"

I look at him, confusion across my brow. Why would the chapters be that far apart? Matt's eyes stay slightly askew. I know he's not drunk, but he's probably buzzed.

"No, wait. Maybe thirty-six and thirty-seven. Yes, thirties, it was definitely in the thirties." He lets out a chuckle, at what I have no idea.

"Damn it, Matt. This is serious." He gives me an apologetic shrug.

Scanning the party, I see our other friend, Lucas. I know he doesn't have Mr. Hilton and neither does Jeremy. I recognize some other people but don't know if they have that class. I could go around asking people, but I'm not a nerd. Not that I have anything against nerds, but I haven't worked two years to become captain of the varsity basketball team and one of the most popular guys in school for nothing. Yeah, yeah, it's shitty and shallow, but I'm not giving up my good rep unless it's absolutely necessary. If it comes down to it, I'll turn it over for a week in New York or Miami, but right now I still have options.

"Dude, what's that guy's name in our class that sits behind you. Craig? No, Carson?"

"Carlos."

"Yeah, Carlos. You had that buddy assignment with him last month, right? Did you guys exchange numbers?" Matt nods. "Text me his number. I'll ask him for the assignment."

"You're gonna do five chapters by tomorrow?"

"The class isn't until the end of the day. I got all night tonight and then tomorrow." Matt looks at me like I'm crazy. "Dude, just do it."

"Fine," he says, reaching for his phone next to him. "There you go."

My phone chirps next to my head and I grab it, sending off the text message.

ME: Hey, Carlos. You don't know me, we're in Mr. Hilton's calculus class and I got your number from Matt. I was hoping I could get the weekend assignment from you. Thanks!

I want to breathe a sigh of relief, but I'm not sure how long it will be until he replies. Hopefully not long. We all look at our phones constantly, right? But maybe he has it on silent. Or maybe he has a limited data plan. Or maybe it broke. Thinking about missing out on my graduation gift starts making the stress levels rise as my phone goes off.

UNKNOWN: This isn't Carlos. Wrong number

I read the screen and shoot Matt an annoyed look. I'm about to tell him when my phone chirps again.

UNKNOWN: Why didn't u do the assignment? It's five chapters long. There's no way you can do that in one night

Wait, what? It's the wrong number, but it's still a student at Woodbridge? How crazy is that? Or maybe it is Carlos, messing with me. I don't really know him, so perhaps he's joking around.

ME: If this isn't Carlos, then how do u know about the assignment?

I stare at my phone. Whoever it is has an iPhone like me, because I can see that they're typing a response.

"Did you get it?" Matt asks, glancing over at me.

"Yeah," I answer, still staring at my phone.

UNKNOWN: Only seniors take Mr. Hilton. Woodbridge has a senior class of over 400.

I give my phone an irked grin.

ME: Fine, thank u for the statistics. Do you know what the assignment is?
UNKNOWN: I do
ME: Well...

And then nothing. I stare at the screen, waiting for a reply, but there's no activity. No message popping up saying they're typing. Finally, growing tired of waiting, I snap my head back over to Matt.

"Dude, that wasn't—" My phone chirps.

UNKNOWN: Chapters 33-35, 38 and 39.

I let out a sigh of relief as I type my response.

ME: Thanks

Before I can look over at Matt, the water in the hot tub moves around, making me lift my arms up to keep my phone out of the water. Sarah Donovan's tanned skin comes into my peripheral, as she slides next to me in the hot tube.

"Hey, Carter." She breathes out the words, in a blatant attempt to be flirty.

Sarah is a knockout, no doubt about it. Light auburn hair, gray eyes that flicker blue in the sunlight. Captain of the cheerleading team. She has the valley girl accent going on, and she's smart. And, as I found out at the beginning of the year, super interested in me. A little too much. I know, what red-blooded guy wouldn't want a hot girl, with legs that went for days, and a great rack that she's brazenly pressing against my arm right now? And it's not that I'm not interested because I was for a little while.

But she's like a yapping chihuahua, always barking to get attention. Actually, no, more like a rottweiler. Sarah can be demanding. She wants what she wants and when she wants it.

Maybe part of it is my fault because I did take her to homecoming. Unlike the rest of my friends though, we didn't go to any after-parties. We'd made a detour into the women's bathroom that night and messed around. If someone hadn't walked in on us, we probably would've had sex in there. Not my proudest moment, especially since I've never considered myself an exhibitionist. The girl who walked in on us quickly excused herself, but Sarah was still ready to go. I had to practically drag her out of the bathroom, to get back to the dance. And by the time it was over, I was over it.

I hooked up with a girl last year, which is what initially started the rumor mill and my ascension in the popularity ranks. So, at homecoming, even though I knew exactly how far we'd gone, I knew the rumors that were out there. Matt's the only one I told the truth to, letting everyone else believe what they wanted. Because believing what they wanted only helped my reputation.

It might sound crazy, but sometimes you don't want the girl throwing herself at you. At least, I didn't. A little mystery went a long way. A little pursuit. With Sarah, the only thing I'd be pursuing was how fast she'd stick her hand down my pants.

Matt looks over at me, as I catch her hand sliding up my board shorts.

"What's up, Sarah?"

"We got here late," she said, faking a pouty face, "but I'm glad I found you."

"Oh yeah?" I say, trying to sound uninterested as Matt wiggles his eyebrows at me.

"Yeah." She pulls her hand free from mine and places it on my chest. "Jeremy said his parents weren't coming back until tomorrow night."

"I know."

Her lips find my ear. "He said he'd let us use his bedroom." She nibbles on my ear, as her hand slid down from my chest into the water, over my stomach.

"Well, isn't he just a super friend." I look past her, over at Jeremy. He's looking back at me, giving me a salute with a cup, no doubt filled with more beer.

Her hand slides lower, her fingers sliding under the waistband of my board shorts. The hot tub has bubbles going, but it isn't like you can't see what she's doing. I push her hand away and stand up.

"Sorry, I actually have a homework assignment I gotta make up before tomorrow." I step out, grabbing my towel, as she looks up at me with her fake pouty lips again. "Matt?"

"Huh," he mumbles.

"Come on, time to go."

Another reason I'm not drinking is I'm our DD. His eyes dart from me back to Sarah, and I know exactly what he's thinking. "You sure?"

"Yeah." I nod as I dry my hair.

Grabbing our shirt and shoes, we walk past Jeremy and Lucas, into the house. A slight tinge of remorse hits me, feeling bad for how abrupt I was with Sarah. Turning around, my sorrow vanishes as I see Sarah already flirting with another guy, but her eyes meet mine and she mouths 'call me'. I let out an incredulous scoff, as I roll my eyes and head to my car.

Chapter 2

Emma

I have a decision to make. Either go with my nearly worn out Converse Chucks or the scuffed-up Doc Martens. Today I feel like doing a throwback to the goth look. Black net stockings, a dark purple skirt that goes down just above my knees, and my favorite Star Wars shirt that has the original movie poster. Sure, it'll be a little chilly outside, but I'm going to be inside most of the day anyway.

I slather on the eyeliner and apply the darkest, reddest, lipstick I have. Okay, I do dab a bit of glitter on my cheeks, but I love that stuff. Now, it's about deciding what shoes to wear. The boots would make the outfit, but my Chucks are so comfy. I hear Jen's horn, honking outside.

Deciding on the boots, I quickly slip them on and grab my backpack, leaving the house. "Bye, Mom!" I yell, without waiting for a reply.

Running out to Jen's Corolla, I fling my backpack in the backseat.

"Hey," she says, pulling out on to the road.

"Ugh!" I groan, already feeling the uncomfortableness of the boots. "I should've gone with my Chucks."

Jen glances down at my feet. "Are those Doc Martens?" I nod. "You're so crazy. You're gonna be stuck in those things all day."

"It went with the outfit." I pull out my phone and start scrolling through Instagram.

"Emma, I'll never understand you."

"What?"

"If you were like me–"

"Yeah, because we all want to be Jennifer Harris." I tease her, twirling my hair with a finger while making my voice super high. 'Hi, I'm Jen. I love sunflowers and macchiatos."

"Bitch." She laughs.

"Right back atchya."

"Anyways, if you were like me, or any other girl, I could understand your statement. Like this morning, it took me ten minutes to decide if I wanted to go with my pink top or that lime green one."

"Glad you chose the pink one, it's cute."

She looks back down at my boots. "But you don't have a typical attire. You dress based on who knows what, which is something I'll never understand."

"That's not true. I just like to be random when it comes to clothes."

"Tell me one thing that's not random about you."

"My Star Wars and Harry Potter shirts."

She nods, pulling to a stop sign. "Okay, I'll give you that." She looks over at my phone. "Oh, did you text back Homework Stranger last night?"

I let out a scoff. I still don't understand why Jen egged me on to reply to whoever texted me. We just finished watching a rom-com movie on Netflix, when I received the text message. Other than being my best friend for the past four years, Jen indulged me in my movie watching habits. She put up with my nerdy choices, like Marvel movies or Harry Potter, but we're both rom-com fans. Right before the credits started rolling was when I got the text.

"No." I return my attention to my phone.

"Why not? We probably know who it is; you should've asked."

"Jen, why? I've got enough friends. I don't need to go making new friends with a complete stranger."

"News flash, Emma. Everyone is a complete stranger until you become friends. That's how it works."

"Whatever. You know what I mean. I still can't believe I texted him for so long."

"So, you think it's a guy?"

"I don't know." I shrug.

I really don't. And I didn't think about it much after she left either. Whoever it was needed the homework assignment, which I know there's no way they're going to be able to get done before class today. Those five chapters took me all weekend. Sure, I went to the art store with Jen on Saturday, but still.

"You should text them. See if they finished."

"No." I give her a confused look. "Why would I do that?"

"I don't know. Who knows, maybe it's someone who's even in the class with you." She pulls into the student parking lot, and once she parks, she turns and stares at me.

"What?" I keep my eyes locked on my phone, now scrolling through Twitter.

"Text, text, text," she says, starting to pound the steering wheel lightly. "Text. Text. Text."

"Ugh, you're so annoying in the morning."

"Only when I don't get my macchiato." She gives me an obnoxious smile. Raising my phone, I quickly turn and take a picture. "Hey, what was that?"

"Snapchat." I laugh, as I grab my bag and leave the car, captioning the picture with 'Without Starbucks, Jen's a freak ;P' and add it to my story. I know she's going to yell at me when she sees it later.

Despite my best efforts, I can't help but look around Mr. Hilton's calculus class, as I walk into the room. It's my first class of the day, so if Mystery Texter did complete the assignment, he or she would probably look somewhat sleepless right about now. Taking my seat, I scan the room, trying to be as subtle as I can about it. Ethan, who sits across from me, quirks an eyebrow.

"What's up?" he asks.

"Hmm? Oh, nothing." I straighten back up in my seat.

Ethan's a nice guy, and we're friendly, but I wouldn't go as far as to call him my friend. It's not like we hang out or anything. Maybe classmate is a better way of describing him, and most of the other seniors in my class. Jen's my best friend, but other than that, I think I can count on one hand the number of people I'm close with in school. Jen's the extrovert of our duo, and I'm the introvert. She always teases me about it, calling me the 'cliché artsy girl' who keeps to herself. Which, I guess is true. But it's not because I'm shy. There are just lots of fake people.

Jocks pretending to be super cool, half of them already the popular kids, acting like big shots. But I've seen what happens to those popular kids at school. The prom kings and queens. My mom was prom queen. Then, one year after high school, she marries my dad, has a baby, and she's been a housewife ever since. Wow, that sounds like I'm trashing my mom, and I don't mean to. I love her. But she's the one who's ingrained it in me ever since I started high school.

"Esmeralda," she said, giving me a serious look as she pulled into the parking lot, my freshman year. "High school can be fun, but don't let what happens here, change who you are. Kids will be kids. Some of them cruel, some stuck up, and some jerks. But high school is only four years. And when it's over, then you find out who you are."

I didn't even try to understand it at the time. I kept nervously looking over my shoulder as Jen waited for me to get out of the car. But over my high school career, that morning has always stuck with me. And I've done what I want to do. I take art classes. I volunteer. I do things that I want to do, even if other people think it's stupid or lame, because like she said, high school is only four years. When it ends, that's when life really begins. It's another reason I've never bothered trying to date anyone at school either. Not that I have a whole line of guys waiting to ask me out.

Which is another thing that Jen and I are opposites on. She loves boys. Okay, I love boys too, but she *really* loves them and has no problem calling herself a flirt. And she tries to get me to go on double dates with her all the time. I tried it a couple of times, but it was obvious the guys were there to try and make a move.

"If you'd just put something normal on," Jen said one time, which led to the biggest fight we've ever had.

She'd convinced me to go out with her and a guy she was dating last year. When she came and picked me up, I was dressed how I always dress; however I want to. I decided to go with some skinny jeans, a crop top, and my Chucks. Hey, I said they're comfy. I guess that would've been *normal* enough, but I topped it off with my Hufflepuff necktie, loosely wrapped around my neck and wore a thick pair of glasses. I usually wear my contacts, but I wanted the nerdy glasses look, which I've always kind of liked.

As the night progressed, my date kept commenting on my tie, asking me to take it off. He kept saying it looked dorky, especially since I 'had to' wear my glasses that night. I ignored him for the rest of the night and by the time we got home–which was earlier than Jen wanted because my date was 'over the night'–she yelled at me.

"What does it matter what I'm wearing? It's just a tie!" I'd yelled back at her.

"And your glasses?"

"Jen, you know I wear glasses."

"Ha!" She exaggerated the sound. "You always wear contacts. Why put on your glasses tonight? And even then, I know I've seen other glasses you have. Why'd you have to wear those? Chad was totally put off."

"I don't care!" I yelled back. "If he gets turned off because I'm wearing glasses, then he's shallower than I thought."

"Shallow?" Jen looked at me like I had slapped her. "Well, I think that too. Does that mean I'm shallow?"

"Jen, you know that's not what I meant."

"Maybe it is! God, Emma! Why do always have to be so … different!"

She stormed out of my room, and we didn't talk for two weeks. She finally came over one night, and we settled everything. She apologized for getting upset, and I apologized for how I'd acted. Because, in reality, I did do it on purpose. I could've worn something normal, but I wore my tie and glasses because I didn't want to have to tell that guy no and be looked at as lame. I didn't like him, and since he was a popular guy, I'm sure not many girls had told him no. But I figured he didn't want to be seen kissing some 'nerd' with a Harry Potter tie and huge glasses. I was right.

After scanning the room one more time, it looks like everyone's turning in their assignment. No tired looks on faces, at least no more than usual. Facing forward, I reach down to my feet. It's been less than an hour, and I already feel my stupid boots hurting.

By the time lunch rolls around, I could feel a blister starting to form under my right big toe. Plopping down next to Jen, I pull out my sandwich and take a bite, while scrolling through my phone.

"So, did you?"

"Did I what?" I answer without looking at her.

"Text them."

"Oh my God, you're still going on about that?"

"Well, did you see anyone who looked like a zombie in first period?" I shake my head, taking a drink of water. "So then text them."

"What for?"

"I don't know, it's weird. How crazy is it that someone randomly texts you, thinking it's someone else, but it's still someone you might know?"

"If anything, *you'd* know them, I wouldn't."

"Hey, you know people," she says as she opens a bag of chips. "Anyways, it's weird though, right? I mean, they could've texted anyone. Someone in Wisconsin or something. But they didn't, so you need to text them."

"Gah, fine!" I drop my shoulders, giving her an exasperated look. "If it'll get you to shut up, I'll text them."

"I love you." A broad smile crosses her lips.

I look down at my phone and suddenly go blank. Why am I nervous to text a complete stranger? What if it's someone I *did* know? Would they want to know me? And why am I analyzing a random text to a stranger so much?

Chapter 3

Carter

My pencil moves furiously, as I scramble it across my paper at our lunch table. I stayed up until three o'clock, working on as much of the assignment as I could before finally going to sleep. I'm going to be dead at practice after school, but I have to make sure the assignment is done.

"Dude." Jeremy looks over the table as he takes a bite of pizza. "I still can't believe you turned down what would've been at least a BJ, to do homework."

"Shut up," I mutter under my breath, scribbling more of the equation I'm working on.

"Don't worry. I made sure my bedroom didn't go to waste."

"I'm sure you did."

"Carter, why don't you copy someone's?" Lucas, who's sitting next to Jeremy, looks over the table at my paper.

"No way." I flip over to the next page. "You heard what

happened last month. Mr. Hilton caught Phillip and Lewis cheating and is docking them down a whole letter grade at the end of the semester. I can't afford to get docked down a letter."

I don't look up, but he must look confused. "His graduation gift," Matt says, sitting next to me.

"Oh, that's right," Lucas replies. "Well, you can at least look at their work, so you're not stressing."

Matt takes a bite of his sandwich. "I told him the same thing," he says with a mouthful.

"No, you guys." I finally look up. "Last week he said we're having a test later this week. It's most likely on all this stuff, and I gotta pass the test too."

"Still, man." Jeremy shoots me a look. "Sarah was looking fine as hell last night. She ended up making out with Scott, I think."

I give Jeremy a deadpan look. "Yeah, and you wonder why it's not a big deal that I don't hook up with her anymore. That girl just gives it away."

Matt snickers as Lucas let out a laugh.

"True." Jeremy nods. "Plus, you already had a piece of that pie earlier this year." He flashes the conceited smile he likes to show.

Jeremy loves to bring up the homecoming incident as if it's a badge of honor. Inwardly, I'm still embarrassed by it, but outwardly, I do joke around about it being awesome. I remember later that night, Jeremy and the rest of our basketball team all high-fiving me. It put me on another level.

Rumors spread quickly that night, and before I knew it, we had committed a number of lewd acts in the women's bathroom, the men's bathroom, and a janitor's closet. I was going to tell Jeremy and Lucas the truth, but by the time school rolled around the following week, my popularity had skyrocketed. After that, more rumors started making their rounds, and with each new one, a new level of popularity was unlocked. A couple of weeks went by, and I couldn't bring myself to tell my friends. I didn't like being so concerned with what people thought about me, but this is high school. Our reputation is, like, what determines our net-worth. And after homecoming, I became worth a whole lot more.

My phone chirps.

UNKNOWN: So'd u finish the assignment?

I grin at the screen, wondering who this person is.

ME: Of course

Hey, no need to tell them I'm still working on it. I decide to ask the mystery texter who they are, wondering if they're even in my class. That'd be weird.

ME: BTW who is this?

I wait for a couple of minutes, but there's no answer. Shrugging my shoulders, I turn back to my book. Only two more pages to complete and I still have a class before calculus.

UNKNOWN: U tell me first
ME: I asked first

First bell rings, letting everyone know lunch is over and it's time to get to class, so I start packing everything up.

Jeremy and Lucas take off, but Matt waits for me since we have our last two classes together. Walking away from the table, my phone chirps.

UNKNOWN: U texted me first. That means I should know who's texting. Plus, I helped u

I stare at my phone with a little annoyance. Even if I did text them first, I'm not going to give this random person my name.

ME: Watevs. Thanks for the help HW-Buddy

I laugh to myself as I head to my next class with Matt.

Chapter 4

Emma

UNKNOWN: Watevs. Thanks for the help HW-Buddy

"What the heck is 'HW-Buddy'?"

Jen glances over my shoulder and shrugs, as we get up from our table. "I don't know. I'll see you later." She waves, as she heads down the hallway to her next class.

ME: ???

I switch my phone to silent in case whoever this is decides to text me during class. I'm still looking at the messages, wondering why exactly I'm exchanging texts with a total stranger. I mean, if they are a senior at Woodbridge, then I guess it's not some forty-year-old guy, but still. I probably should end this soon.

I'm about to slide my phone into my pocket when I feel

the blister on my toe again and cringe in pain. Then someone shouts, as I slam against a chest.

"Whoa." Carter Dixon is standing in front of me, between myself and the door to our classroom.

"Ew." I look up at him, annoyed.

"Excuse me?" He curls a lip. "You walked into me. Of course, I could've let you keep going and run right into the metal door." He knocks his knuckles against the door. "You seemed to be distracted. I saw you behind me and opened the door, but you kept walking."

"Oh." I look around. A few students look over, noticing the exchange.

Carter Dixon is one of those cool kids I was talking about. He's got light brown hair, with eyes to match, and a pearly white smile that unleashes a cute dimple. Yes, he's gorgeous, but he's also one of the popular kids. Which means, he tries to act cooler then he probably is. Although to be fair, I don't really know him.

I only really know three things about Carter. One - he's the captain of the varsity basketball team, and I just found out first hand, that all that time shooting basketballs has given him a firm chest and stomach. Something I can also see, as his T-shirt fits snuggly against his chest. Two - he's friends with Jeremy McCormick, who acts like he's God's gift to women and has the ego to match. I have two classes with Jeremy and cringe every time he makes a 'that's what she said' joke. It's like he waits on the edge of his seat for the teacher to say something–anything–that would be the slightest bit applicable to that joke. And three - Carter probably had sex with Sarah Donovan in the women's restroom at homecoming.

Rumor has it, he's the biggest manwhore at Woodbridge. Hey, I'm not slut shaming anyone. Jen, who I know has had sex and is kind of boy crazy, is my best friend. I don't think any less of her. But imagining Carter with half the girls in our senior class is gross, no matter how hot he is. Hence, my reaction to bumping into him.

"Yeah, 'oh'." He gives me a confident grin.

"Well, thanks." I try to give him a cordial smile, but it vanishes as I see his eyes roam from my face to my chest. He tries to play it off, his eyes flicking back up to meet mine, but I already saw it. Rolling my eyes, I walk into the classroom. Gross.

As I take my seat, I pull out my phone, taking a quick glance at my text messages, but they haven't replied. Mrs. Yanick starts handing out packets of our next subject, covering the Civil War, and I see Carter on the other side of the room. He's writing something down before he even gets his packet. I scrunch my eyebrows, wondering if he knows what the assignment is already. I've heard some of the jocks know what certain assignments are going to be, so they can work on them before whatever game they're playing.

By the time history is over, I let out a sigh of relief. Art is my last class of the day, and since Ms. Hales has been my art teacher all four years, it's become somewhere I let my hair down. I still do all my work, but it also it doesn't feel like work to me. And since it's Ms. Hales, I plan on finally slipping out of my boots. I don't even care if my socks stink.

Right before I get to the door, my phone chimes.

UNKNOWN: Homework-Buddy. Since u won't tell me your name

I give my phone an incredulous stare.

ME: My name isn't HW-Buddy either

UNKNOWN: So, what do I call you?

Walking into art class, I drop my bag by my easel and look back at my phone, unsure what to say next.

ME: Um…

I roll my eyes at my lame answer. As if thinking the same thing, they answer with a snarky reply.

UNKNOWN: Okay, Um. Nice to meet you. I've never met anyone named Um. Is it foreign?

Even though it's snarky, it's funny, and a smile cracks my lips. But the reply is still dumb.

ME: Don't be a jerk
UNKNOWN: Oh! Ur a girl!

"Emma, class is about to start," Ms. Hales says.

"Sorry." I put my phone away, but now I'm even more intrigued. How do they know I'm a girl? Does that mean they're a girl? What if it's a boy? Is it a boy I know?

Chapter 5

Carter

I spend the entire time in history working on my calculus assignment and finish it just before the bell rings. I may get a little behind in history, but nothing I can't make up. I'm pretty confident that my calculus work is all good too, so I'm all smiles as we leave the classroom.

Matt nudges my elbow, pointing at Emma Sanchez walking out. Running into me isn't the worst thing that could've happened. She's pretty and not to sound like a douche, but she could be hot if she tried. But she doesn't try. She wears what she wants and doesn't care what other people think of her. You have to respect that on some level. We both watch as she walks out the door, her purple skirt covering over nylon stockings. Okay, I retract my previous statement. That's hot. And her Star Wars shirt covers her curves perfectly. Or maybe I'm remembering her chest bumping into me.

I give Matt an agreeing nod, as we leave class and head to calculus. On the way there I reply to my mystery texter, and I'm almost positive it's a girl.

See, they called me a jerk. Now, this isn't a scientific theory, more of a hunch. I don't think a guy would say that. But the last text I sent was telling them I thought they're a girl and haven't received a reply. I wonder if it is and I scared them off?

Mr. Hilton walks around and collects all of our assignments, and I happily hand mine over. Getting through the last class of the day goes by slow, and I can't wait for the bell to ring, eagerly anticipating practice.

I love basketball. And while most people in the LA area are Lakers fans, I'm a Clippers fan. After my dad left, my mom took me to as many games as she could. It's something I'll always remember fondly and appreciate, not only because I always looked at it like it was our bonding time, but she knows next to nothing about basketball. All she knew was that I liked basketball, and Clippers tickets were cheaper than Lakers tickets, so that's where we went.

As soon as the bell rings to end the school day, my phone chirps.

UNKNOWN: Excuse me?

I grin, still almost positive it's a girl. I look around the hallway, seeing several girls on their phone. I wonder who it is. Maybe it's someone I know. Someone I thought was hot.

ME: You called me a jerk. A dude would've called me an asshole or dick, but u said jerk. Hence, girl.

Smiling, the typing prompt appears on my screen. But

the longer the typing message is there, the more I begin to feel a little weird. Is it wrong to assume they're a girl, based on a word? I mean, I have girl friends who curse all the time.

UNKNOWN: Fine, yes. I am a girl... But that must mean you're a chauvinistic waste of the male population
ME: And proud! ;)
UNKNOWN: Disgusting >:\

I smile again, making my way to our locker room.

ME: So...
ME: What's ur name?
UNKNOWN: I'm not giving u my name.
ME: Then what should I call u?
UNKNOWN: What should I call YOU?
ME: BigBaller27 ;P

I chuckle at myself as I open my locker and pull out my jersey. Maybe I'm being a little too revealing, putting my basketball number as my handle. No, first they'd have to watch our games, and even though we have a few good players, we don't win much. Plus, twenty-seven could be anything. A day of the month. Whatever.

UNKNOWN: Didn't need much time for that.
UNKNOWN: What r u? Some rich kid?
UNKNOWN: OMG! This isn't Tommy Harrison, is it?

I know who Tommy is. A rich kid, but his parents live in Woodbridge, so he still goes to school with us. He has a few friends, but they all act superior to everyone else because they have money. Jeremy could be a dick at times, but at least he didn't act like he was too good for us.

BigBaller27: Y? U got a thing for Tommy?

The bubble that shows them typing pops up, then it goes blank. It appears again, then blank again. She's definitely trying to think of the right thing to say, in case this is Tommy. I decide to play it cool and put her mind at ease.

BigBaller27: Relax. I'm not ur crush
UNKNOWN: Ew, gross X(

The response makes me laugh again. Even though I have no idea who this person is, it also calms something that I didn't realize I'm feeling. Why am I relieved that a girl I don't know and have only talked to for one day, doesn't like a douchebag like Tommy Harrison? Putting my phone in my locker, I head out to practice.

First practices of the week are usually pretty brutal, except when we have a game the next day, which we do. After running a few drills, we go over plays that worked for us, and stuff we didn't execute properly at our last game, which we barely won.

I'm the team captain and starting shooting guard. Jeremy plays center, Lucas is our point guard, and Matt's our backup power forward. It sucked at the beginning of the season, learning we all made the starting lineup, except Matt, but as usual with him, he rolled with the punches.

"I'm still playing." He laughed after the starters were announced.

Even though he played it cool, I could tell it bugged him. It bothered me too because he isn't even much of a basketball fan. He's been a starting wide-receiver for our varsity football team since he was a sophomore. And he's our class president. He only joined the basketball team because I asked him too.

After practice, we hit the showers and Jeremy tells us about a party happening this weekend.

"Dude, you just had a party." I look at him, wrapping a towel around my waist, heading for my locker.

"Yeah, but this isn't my party. It's Tamara Winston's." He wiggles his eyebrows.

Tamara is one of the rich kids, who lives near Jeremy. I nod, opening my locker and remember my text message because Tamara is friends with Tommy. I wonder if my texter has replied.

UNKNOWN: Emerald22

I look at the screen, confused.

BigBaller27: What's that?
UNKNOWN: That's what you can call me.

After putting on my clothes and locking up my locker, I edit her contact info.

BigBaller27: Okay, Dorothy :P
Emerald22: It's not about Wizard of Oz.
BigBaller27: My bad

I slip my phone into my pocket and head out to my car in the student parking lot, for some reason with a feeling of accomplishment. I'm talking to a girl, I have no idea who she is, and don't even know what she looks like. Crazy.

There are only a few cars left in the lot. Across the way, some cheerleaders are on the football field going over routines. I don't want to linger too long since I know Sarah is probably over there somewhere, but I wonder if Emerald22 is out there. Is she a cheerleader? Is she in any of my classes?

Chapter 6

Emma

"What's Emerald22?" Jen asks as we hang out in my room.

"Well, emerald is my birthstone."

"And your birthday is May 22nd. Clever." She smiles as she scrolls through Instagram.

"Are you staying for dinner?"

"I don't know." She looks at her phone a little closer. "This might be him."

I look over her shoulder at her screen, as we both lay on top of my bed. It's open to the profile of a guy that kind of looks familiar. His profile says his name is Steve. Under that, it reads 'Livin' Large in So Cal $$$'.

"Steve?" I ask.

"Yeah, Steven Perez, I think? He hangs out with Tamara and all them."

"Hmm." I examine the screen. "He's kinda cute."

She shrugs. "Meh. But if he hangs out with the richies, he's most likely a dick."

"Jen!" I glare at her. She returns it to me. "Yeah, you're probably right. I think Big Baller is nice though. At least, nice at heart."

"And you would know this how?"

"I don't know," I say, sitting up. "I mean, who asks for a homework assignment? He could've copied from one of his friends or something."

She closes the app and sits up. "I guess so. Still kind of a stupid name. Big Baller? I mean, come on!"

I let out a little chuckle. I agree with her, and I said the same thing when he texted that, but it is funny. Oh God, what am I doing?

"This is stupid." I get up from my bed. "Why am I wondering who he is? He probably won't text again. I know I won't."

"You won't?" Jen gives me a mischievous smile.

"No. I mean, I shouldn't. It's dumb. I don't even know him."

"Stop."

I stop and look at her, suddenly realizing I'm pacing my room. "Sorry."

"If he did text you again though, what would you say?"

I stare at her, and my mind goes blank. What would I say? I guess it depends on what he'd say. Then I shake my head again, for what feels like the millionth time today. *Why am I freaking out about this so much?* As if reading my mind, Jen speaks up.

"It's cuz you like him." She smirks.

"What?" I stare at her with a deadpan expression. "Jen, that's insane. I don't even know him."

"But you're getting to know him. Or at least, you want to.

I can tell. You already made that homework comment. He's probably smart, so that already gets you going. I know how you like the nerds."

I hold up a finger. "First of all, that's rude. I'm a nerd."

"No, you're not. You're ... eccentric."

"Same thing. And secondly, how is texting him for one day–"

"A day and a half."

"Whatever. How is that getting to know him?"

"You know he needed—or wanted—to do his home-work. So, he's at least somewhat smart. He's got money or likes to think he does, with a handle like that. He teased you about liking Tommy, which kind of means he may like you to."

"What?"

"You know, how like in grade school the boys would tease you at recess if they liked you."

"I always stayed inside during recess."

"Of course, you did. Anyways, the most important part, you found out he's a boy." She wiggles her eyebrows.

"Don't be gross."

"Hey, just because you don't date, doesn't mean you don't think about those things. I know you do, Emma."

"Hey, I date." I scold her.

"The last date you went on was with me, last year when you pulled that glasses and tie stunt. You didn't even want to be there. I don't think that qualifies as dating."

"So, I don't date all the time."

"Never."

"It's just because I have priorities. Plus, most of the guys at school are stupid. Stupid high school boys." I fold my arms, daring her to counter my argument.

"But–"

"No buts."

"Oh!" She grins. "I wonder if he's got a cute butt."

"You're so stupid." I laugh, as my mom calls out that dinner's ready.

Jen ends up staying over for my mom's dinner, which is enchiladas. She makes this amazing green sauce that's to die for. While we're eating, I glance at my phone a few times, and Jen notices it on more than one occasion. She finally bumps my leg under the table and motions to my phone, but I shake my head that I haven't received any texts.

By the time dinner's over, Jen goes home, and I hang out with my parents for a little while, as we watch TV and forget about my phone. Later, as I'm getting ready for bed, I plug it into the charger and open my text messages. The last exchange was him saying 'my bad'. Maybe he thought I was mad when I said my name didn't have anything to do with *Wizard of Oz*. I didn't mean it in a bad way, but I didn't add any emojis or anything. Those always lighten up the conversation. Or maybe he forgot about me.

Putting my phone back on my nightstand, I stare up at the dark ceiling. Maybe it's for the best. He may go to my school, but he could be some freak. But I don't think he's a freak. What kind of freak cracks jokes and asks for homework assignments. Letting out a deep breath, I try to forget everything and will myself to sleep.

As soon as I wake up, I grab my phone out of habit. I'd be lying if I said I wasn't a little disappointed to see I had no new text messages. *Why? Why am I disappointed?* After scrolling my usual social media apps, as I do every morning, I finally get up and get ready for school. Looking through my closet, my Chucks are the first thing I decide to wear today. My glorious, comfy Chucks.

When we first get to school, I find myself eyeing

everyone on campus. Everyone I walk by in the student parking lot, as I get out of Jen's car. Everyone in the hallway. I even start scanning Mr. Hilton's class again, since that's the only class I know he has. But no one looks familiar. Which sounds dumb, but I thought I might be able to match up a face, just by the few texts I'd received. I know, I know. Dumb.

By the time second period comes around, I start to forget about the messages. My sound reasoning comes back, and I know it's for the best. Are we going to fall madly in love through text messages, and then reveal ourselves to each other at prom? Yeah, right. This was a stupid coincidence, and I know I should get on with life.

Pulling out my sandwich for lunch, I slide next to Jen at the table we usually sit at in the quad. The tables here are a little further out then the main lunch area tables, so it's not as noisy.

"Hey," I say, unwrapping my sandwich.

"Jeez, I thought your mood would be better than this morning, but it's worse."

"What?" I gape at her. "My mood is fine, thank you very much."

"No new texts?"

"No." Now I'm painfully aware of how grumpy I sound. "Sorry, I shouldn't be as bummed out about it as I am. It's stupid, right? I don't even know him."

I do a quick glance around, making sure I didn't say it loud enough for someone else to hear. Micah and Lana, who usually sit with us, haven't shown up yet, so I feel a little more comfortable talking about it.

"It's not stupid," she says before taking a drink of her Diet Coke. "It's like when a guy asks for your number and doesn't call. It sucks."

"But he didn't ask for my number, Jen."

"No, he already has it. So, don't feel bad. He's being a jerk. It's what guys do."

Her comments should make me feel better, but they don't. I take another bite of my sandwich, doing a quick scan of the area, checking out the guys that walk by. Any of them could be him, and I don't have a clue. I let out a defeated huff, wishing I wasn't thinking about this so much. Then my phone chimes.

Jen's eyes widen at me, a smile creeping across her lips.

I try to fight off a smile. "No. It's probably a tweet or a snap."

As I pull out my phone, for some reason my heart flutters. I have my phone set to show I've received a text message, but it stays private until I open my messages. I try to keep calm, because who knows, maybe it's my mom asking what I want to have for dinner. Even if she's never texted me for that. Opening up my messages, I can't stop the smile that appears.

"It is!" Jen shouts.

"What is?" Micah says as he and Lana show up.

"Nothing," I mutter, glancing at Jen to not say anything.

We've exchanged enough silent conversations that she knows when I want to keep something a secret. Micah and Lana are our friends, Micah's in art too, and Lana is his girlfriend. We're close, but I don't tell them everything like I do with Jen. Maybe I will if this goes any further, but right now I still want to find out exactly what this is.

BigBaller27: Where do u sit for lunch?
Emerald22: At a table

I smile at my joke, before taking another bite of my lunch.

BigBaller27: Ha. Ha. Ha. <--- Fake laugh. Seriously...

Emerald22: Why do u want to know?

BigBaller27: Idk, maybe I want to buy you a soda ;)

Emerald22: With all that big baller money? And u should probably get a name from a girl before u go asking her out for a drink ;P

BigBaller27: Oh. Are u giving me ur name finally? And I wasn't asking you "out for a drink". Not unless you want me to

I feel my face go red and immediately slide my phone in my pocket. Oh my God, what am I doing? Did he just ask me if I wanted him to ask me out?

Chapter 7

Carter

By the time lunch is over, I still haven't received a reply from Emerald22. I'm starting to feel a little bad. I have no idea who she is, and I was joking around ... for the most part. I was hoping she would give me the general area of where she sits for lunch, and I could walk by, scanning the faces. But then I had to make that 'going out' comment. She didn't even know me. She could think I was some weirdo or something. And why in the hell was I joking around about asking a girl out, when I don't even know what she looks like?

Matt kept giving me weird looks throughout lunch and history class, but I told him I was nervous about the game tonight. That answer came with another odd stare from him because I never get nervous about the games. I feel bad about lying to him, but even if he's my best friend, I wasn't ready to tell him I have a ... what do I have?

If you'd have asked me two days ago, I'd say a wrong

number. After yesterday, I thought maybe I'd made a new friend. But after my stupid text earlier, now my mind is racing. Am I interested in this girl?

I'm glad our shoot-around practice before our home game is something that can take my mind off the messages. The court is one of the places I feel most comfortable. Setting my phone in my locker, I take one last look at it. I feel like I have to clear the air at least. It's been nearly two hours since my text, and I haven't heard anything.

BigBall27: Hey, sorry about that last message. I was just screwing around :/

I look at the phone, hoping a reply would show up fast, but it doesn't. Locking my locker, I head out to the court and miss nearly half my shots during the shootaround.

"What the hell is wrong with you?" Jeremy jogs over to me.

"Nothing." I scowl at him, before seeing Matt glance at me. Whatever he's thinking, he keeps it to himself.

"You're shooting like shit. I know Oceanview sucks, but we ain't bringing home any championships either."

"I know, Jer."

"And we've gotten off to a good start this season. We might make the playoffs this year if we stay focused."

"I said I know."

Lucas runs over to us and eyes me suspiciously but doesn't say anything. He looks at Matt, silently asking him what gives, and Matt shrugs his shoulders. Jeremy and I exchange stares for a moment longer, then Coach Hallinan yells at us.

"I don't know if you guys know this, but you actually have to *play* basketball. That means running, shooting,

guarding. Not standing around on the court, like a bunch
of asses!"

I look over at coach and wave my hand as an apology,
catching up with the rest of the team. Blocking all distrac-
tions, I focus on the ball. On the net. On the defender I'm up
against. Soon enough, I leave my cell phone, and my stupid
text messages in the background and the game is front and
center.

After the shoot-around, we head back to the lockers. I'm
so annoyed with how I shot, that I quickly change and don't
even look at my phone. Jeremy makes a stupid comment
about keeping our focus, making sure it's loud enough that I
hear. I'm the captain of the team, but he likes to act like he's
the leader of all of us, on and off the court. It can be annoying, but I know I run things when it's game time. Ignoring
him, I walk out to the parking lot, anxious to get home and
relax before the game tonight.

"Yo, hold up," Matt calls after me.

Opening the door, I fling my bag inside, and then
scratch at the chipped paint on the roof my used Honda. It
was Mom's before she surprised me by handing over the
keys to me when I got my license. She'd secretly been saving
up to buy herself a new car, nothing fancy, but a new one
nonetheless so that I could have the Honda. Besides a few
spots where the paint was chipping, it was in decent shape.
And it had an AC, which is vital in Southern California.

"What's up, man?" Matt opens the passenger side door to
his car, a Lexus, that's parked next to mine.

"Nothing."

"Come on." He gives me a look that I've seen before. A
look that tells me he knows I'm lying. "You started acting
weird at lunch, almost like you were nervous. And you were
definitely not okay in there." He points back to the gym.

Staring down at the pavement, I debate with myself on whether or not to tell him. I don't think he'll laugh, or say anything stupid, but *I* still didn't know what's going on. I'll let him know if things start to get interesting. If I start to like this girl. I can't like her right now, can I? I didn't even know her name.

"Dude, it's all good. Other than Jeremy acting a dick on the court, per usual."

Matt lets out a laugh, but he still gives me a suspicious look. "Yeah, I can't believe he's still not over you being named the captain and not him."

"It's like whatever." I shrug it off. "Anyways, I'll see you back here in a couple of hours."

I give him a fist bump as he gives me one last wary look, before hitting my fist. "Yeah, sure."

Sitting in my car, I pull out my phone. If I'm tripping this much over a few text messages, this isn't worth it. I'm just going to delete the whole conversation and hope she doesn't text me back. That'll put an end to it.

Turning my phone on, a new text message alert pops up. I bite my lip, unsure what it's going to read.

Emerald22: No worries. And ur not getting my name, or any dates for that matter, until I get yours ;)

And there it is. My fear is gone, and I'm smiling as I re-read the text message. Who is this girl? My text didn't freak her out. Or maybe it did, but she's not letting on from the response. It had to be friendly, right? Even a little flirty? She could've ended it after 'no worries', but she added the name thing. And the *date thing*. Something that she didn't have to do. Okay, this wasn't ending anytime soon.

Chapter 8

Emma

As soon as I read the text message, I hide it from Jen. She hounds me during lunch, asking what he wrote, but I can't show here. Especially with Micah and Lana sitting with us. A boy is putting it out there if I want to go out with him. And, of course, I react the way I always do. I turn into a big ball of nerves because I've put boys out of my mind. I don't need to get involved with any stupid games involving guys. But it's moments like these that make me wish I was as comfortable with guys as Jen is.

Last year, before my horrific double date, there was a guy that I thought was cute. Paxton. He was a senior, and we had art together. He had the bad-boy look, complete with leather bracelets, fingernails painted black, torn jeans, and hair hanging in front of his eyes; his bangs always a different color. He was thinner but still defined. I know, because when he'd reach up to help Ms. Hales rearrange frames or easels, I'd sneak a peek as his shirt lifted up. I had to keep myself from drooling on more than one occasion.

But, of course, I was pathetic. I'd been asked out precisely one time before that. I always kept my nose to the ground, consciously avoiding everyone. But at Jen's behest, I decided to put myself out there a little more starting my junior year. And I got noticed right away. I didn't like the first boy who asked me out, so even though I had no idea what was happening—he asked me at lunch, in front of everyone—I smiled and said, "Thanks, but I'm busy." My answer didn't seem to affect him very much, and I thought the way I handled it was entirely appropriate. Jen, on the other hand, scolded me for a week straight, saying how I should've at least gone out with him once. I didn't like him, but Paxton was a different story.

Then it happened. It was the day before winter break, and after art, he walked me to my next class. I was already having a mild panic-attack, even though I'd talked to him a little during class. But this wasn't class. He could've been anywhere, but he was next to me, asking me what kind of things I liked outside of school. Looking back on it, I was so lame. Someone asks you a question, and you answer, right? No big deal. But my stupid brain kept thinking *Oh my God, Paxton's talking to me. Is he flirting with me? Should I flirt back? How do I flirt back? Should I touch his arm? No, wait, laugh at what he says.*

Everything Jen had ever told me about how to 'play the game' when going out with a boy flew through my mind. So, by the time we turned the corner, and I arrived at my next class, I just stood there, staring up at his gorgeous amber eyes.

"Emma?" he said, and I nodded with a huge, dumb, smile on my face. "Emma, did you hear what I said?"

"Oh." I let out a soft giggle and touched his arm.

He looked down at my hand and then back at my face, confused. "Hey, are you okay?"

"What do you mean?" I asked, finally putting together the words he was saying.

"I just asked you out."

"Oh!" I shouted, making some students around us turn and stare. "Oh." Getting myself under control, I remembered Jen telling me you shouldn't seem too anxious. I let out a very calm, "Yeah, that'd be cool."

"Okay." He looked at me again, and though I didn't think it at the time, looking back on it, he was looking at me like I had escaped a mental institution.

He got my number, but I never heard from him the entire two weeks of winter break. When I got back to school, I didn't bring it up, and neither did he. He acted like I was just another classmate he was in art with.

So, even if a guy isn't asking me out, but just bringing up the possibility of me going out with him, I get totally flustered and don't know how to respond. So, I don't.

But that doesn't mean it isn't on my mind. I sit through my entire history class, trying to pay attention, but instead thinking of how to reply. I don't want to shut the door on him completely. He's the one who initiated texting again, asking where I sit for lunch. He's the one that brought up bringing me a soda. He's the one putting it out there. Even if I'm not ready to meet him and find out exactly who he was, I don't want to say no. But I have no idea *what* to say.

Even through art class, it's still scrambling my brain. We're doing life drawing and today is the ever-ready and always dependable, bowl of fruit, but I can't even focus on it. I tried sketching the bowl, the apples and pears, and it all looks like garbage. Or maybe's it's great, but I can't think straight. It's been nearly two hours, and I have no clue what to reply.

As I meet Jen at her car, she hounds me about the text message again, and I finally cave, showing her my phone.

"Oh, my God!" She reaches for the phone, but I keep a death lock on it. "He practically asked you out."

"I know!"

"No, Emma. This is a good thing. It can be like a blind date or something." She claps her hands, totally giddy.

"Jen, this is horrible!" She shoots me a frown. "You know how I am. You know what happened last year with Paxton. I'm no good at these things."

"Well, fine." She lets out a huff, putting her keys in the ignition. "Tell him you're not interested then."

"But—" I stop myself, but it's too late.

Jen's eyes jump to me, a newly excited grin on her lips. "You *are* interested!"

"I can't believe this. I don't even know the guy. But from these texts, he seems nice. Maybe I could be interested, but I have no clue how to react. I'm not like you; my brain turns to mush when it comes to this stuff."

Even though she pushes my buttons from time to time, and yeah, I want to strangle her on occasion, Jen knows my limits.

"Emma, calm down. Let me see your phone." I shoot her a concerned look, the death lock still engaged on my phone. "I'll put it out there for you."

"No way!"

My phone chimes.

BigBaller27: Hey, sorry about that last message. I was just screwing around :/

"Oh, no." I groan as I read the message to her.

"Wait, isn't this what you wanted? He practically took it back."

"That's not what I wanted." I let out a defeated sigh. "Okay, I don't want to go out on a date with him, *right now*. But maybe, I don't know, in the future. I wanted to have that possibility."

Jen's eyebrows scrunch together, and I can tell she's thinking of something. "Gimme your phone."

"No."

"Emma, seriously. Just let me read the whole conversation. I promise I won't reply unless you approve it."

Giving her an unconvinced stare, I slowly hold my hand out. She reaches over to take my phone, but my fingers stay clasped around it. "You promise?"

"I promise."

It's weird, watching her scroll through my messages. She nods a little, raising her eyebrows a couple of times as if she's digesting the conversation and coming up with a plan. I start fidgeting with my fingers, getting more anxious.

"Okay." She taps a finger to her lips. "He does come off kind of nice, when you read the whole thing in context."

"Okay?"

"So, I think he was serious. At lunch. But then you took forever to reply, so he freaked out. I would too if I threw something like that out there and the boy didn't reply."

"Not helping."

"But, I don't know if he really wanted to take it back. He just wanted to make sure you're cool, you know?" I nod, her answer somehow making sense. "So, I'm gonna type—"

"No!" I lunge for my phone.

"Stop," she says with a laugh, keeping me at bay with one

arm. "Listen, I'm going to type a reply, and I'm not going to send it unless you say it's okay. All right?"

I nervously chew on the inside of my lip, as I give her an uneasy nod of approval.

She begins typing and talking out loud as she does. "'No worries. And you're not getting my name, *or any dates for that matter,*'" she emphasizes those words as she's smiling, "'until I get yours.' And I'm adding a winky-smiley face."

She turns the phone around, and I read it to myself. It sounds good. It's simple and friendly, but it's still a little flirty. I smile at her, letting out a sigh of relief.

"Good?" she asks.

"That's perfect."

"Okay." She looks back at the phone, hits send, and hands it back to me. "There."

"Jen, you're a lifesaver."

She laughs as she starts up her car. "Of course, I am. We should get those little two-way radios, that we can put in our ears. That way, when do you go out with Mystery Boy, I can help you."

"Yeah." I laugh with her, as we head out on the road.

That does sound like a good idea, and lord knows I could use as much of Jen's help as I can get, but there's a little piece inside that tells me I need to get it together. I haven't even met this guy, and I'm freaking out. I need to start playing it cool.

And then it hits me. I don't need to play anything. That's how I ended up like this in the first place, trying to play these stupid dating games. So, as we drive to my house, I decide. I'm going to be who I am. I'm not going to try and be flirty like Jen because that's not me. And if Big Baller doesn't like it, then it's his loss.

Of course, all those plans go out the window when I

don't hear back from him for the next two hours. As I sit at home, I can't help but reach for my phone every five minutes, anticipating what he'll reply with. I try to distract myself with homework, but it's no use. I end up regularly checking my phone, then try to distract myself with the internet, before rechecking my phone. Until, finally, I get a reply.

BigBaller27: Well, then, we seem to be at an impasse. How do I know ur not some crazy chick who'll stalk me, if I give u my name? :D

I take a deep breath, reminding myself just to be me. To treat him like a friend.

Emerald22: I could say the same about u lol
BigBaller27: Fair enough. We can still text though.
Emerald22: Yeah. Who knows when you'll need another homework assignment :')
BigBaller27: Or, u know... just to talk :)

I can't help the warmth that spreads inside. Or the smile floating across my lips. I'm physically unable to stop it. He wants to talk. I realize that this could be the best thing possible. Do I like him? Maybe. But I don't have to see him. I don't have to try to be all flirty or play games. I can talk to him and do it through text. Yeah, some things get lost in translation with text messages, but for the most part, I can get to know him. And he can get to know me.

Emerald22: I'd like that :)

Chapter 9

Carter

I must look like an idiot as I'm driving home. I'm beaming. Absolutely beaming. I was so nervous before I sent the message about just talking. I have no idea who she is, what she looks like or sounds like. I don't know if she's tall or short. Is she curvy or stick thin? I have no freaking clue but exchanging the texts with her has lit something inside. I'd never thought I'd try getting to know someone without knowing what they looked like. Maybe this will be a good thing. And the way she comes across in her text messages, she seems like she's cool.

After texting a little more, we set some ground rules. We aren't exchanging names, first of all. We can talk about our classes, but we aren't going to tell each other what period the class is, so we'll still have no idea when each other will be there. Also, we'll only do text messages. Prohibiting phone calls means we won't know what the other one sounds like.

The more rules we put down, the more I can't believe I'm doing this. I'm going to have to tell Matt about this, but I'm not sure how the others will react. Jeremy will bust my balls for sure, especially with Sarah always hanging over me. I push the thought from my mind because this is something entirely different. I can use something different.

I'm about to tell her I have to go because of my basketball game when I think better of it. She might be able to narrow down who I am if I tell her I'm on the team. I decide just to say I have to go, but I'll text her later.

When I get back to the gym, my mood has done a one-eighty, and Matt notices right away.

"Someone's feeling better," he says, as we change into our uniforms.

"I told you. I'm fine."

"Yeah, right. Something was bothering you earlier." He stares at me for a minute, letting his words hang in the air.

I look around the locker room, then back at Matt. "Okay, yeah, something was up. But it's cool now. I'm good."

"What was it?"

Matt's my best friend. He has been for four years. If I had to guess which of my friends wouldn't make a big deal out of what I'm doing, it would be him. But I'm not ready to tell him yet.

"It's ... complicated."

"Dude, come on." He gives me a pleading look.

"I'll tell you, but not right now. It's ..." I think about it. Is it weird? I guess it is, but it's also interesting. Different. "Unconventional."

Matt raises an eyebrow. "Dude, are you–" he looks

around at the locker room and then back at me, mouthing the word gay.

"What?" I scrunch my nose at him.

"I mean, it's cool if you are. I would never have guessed it. Though, now all the avoiding Sarah thing makes more sense."

"Dude, I'm not gay," I say a little too loud and a team-mate behind us, Franco, starts snickering. "Shut up, Franco."

"Whatever," he mumbles, continuing to laugh.

"Anyways." I look back at Matt. "No, I'm not gay. And I've been ducking Sarah, because I'm over that, especially after that fiasco at homecoming. No, this new thing is different, that's all."

"Okay, you're way too secretive here. You gotta tell me."

"I will." I stand up, tucking in my jersey. "Later."

"Okay, boys." Coach comes into the locker room and gathers us all around.

He goes on about remembering to stick to our game plan, which players to keep an eye out for, and everything that he usually goes over. Oceanview High School isn't a great team, but that doesn't mean they're going to be easy to beat. Our basketball team hasn't made the playoffs in three years. But this year we've started out okay and have only lost to one team in our division, so we're hoping to keep up the strong play and shoot for the playoffs this year. Of course, that was the first half of the season, and in the second half, we have harder teams we were going to be facing.

By the time we get courtside, we're all riled up and ready for the game. Our basketball team isn't as good as our lacrosse team, and definitely not as good as our baseball team, and the crowd makes that obvious. We have some students in the stands, along with parents, and a few others, but it's far from a ruckus crowd.

We get off to a hot start, and we're moving the ball around pretty good. By the end of the first quarter, we're up by seven points. Things get better in the second quarter, when we nearly double our score, and keep Oceanview to only nine points, increasing our lead by seventeen.

"That's what I'm talking about!" Jeremy shouts as we make our way to the locker room for halftime.

"Don't get cocky," I say, as he slings his arm over my shoulder.

"Dude, we got this!"

"No, Dixon's right," Coach says, stepping in front of us. "You're playing solid defense. Moving the ball around great, but don't let up. You may have a big lead now, but if you mess around, they will come back on us."

Coach goes over a few plays we'll be running to start the third quarter before he head out back to the court. Things start out good, scoring a quick six points, but Oceanview begins mount come back.

Lucas drives to the hoop, trying to split between two defenders, but has the ball stolen. Jeremy chases them down, but he isn't fast enough. Instead of letting the guy score, Jeremy fouls him, sending him to the free-throw line. They add another point, and now our seventeen-point lead is only a nine-point lead.

Coach calls a timeout, drawing up a play, as we prepare to get the ball back.

"You're on your last foul," I call over to Jeremy.

"I got this." He ignores me, getting the ball from the referee to toss it in.

Throwing it to Lucas, he takes the ball down the court. He passes the ball to Matt, who drives to the basket. Jeremy steps to the side to throw a block for him but isn't in position in time. Instead, Jeremy grabs the defender's arm, pulling him down. A whistle blows and the referee motions, calling a foul on Jeremy.

"That's bullshit!" Jeremy yells at the official.

"Calm down, man," Lucas says, running over to him.

Over the PA system, the announcers for the game relate to the crowd it's Jeremy's sixth foul, which puts him out of the game.

He's still complaining, while Lucas tries to move him off the court.

"Damn it," I grunt, walking over to him.

"That's a shit call, man."

"You grabbed the guy's arm. It was blatant."

"Whatever." He blows me off, waving a hand in my face as our coach comes over.

"Hopkins, you're in," he says.

The rest of the quarter is tight. Oceanview gets the ball back after the foul and outscores us for the next five minutes, cutting down our lead to three points. With ten seconds left in the game I hit a three-pointer and bump our lead back up to six points, before the buzzer rings, ending the game.

Back in the locker room, the coach says a few things about the game, tells us good job and lets us shower.

"Way to go out there." I shoot Jeremy a sarcastic look.

"Whatever." He pulls off his jersey. "We won, didn't we?"

"If that was another team, we might not have."

"Okay, guys," Matt says next to me.

Jeremy raises us his hands, looking around at everyone. "Okay, my bad. My bad." Looking back at me, he gives me a cocky grin. "Maybe I should've gotten whatever you took to turn your shooting around from this afternoon."

"What?"

"What was it? Sarah come over and blow you. Or you rub one out?"

"Screw you." I scowl at him as laughs.

It's times like these I wonder why I'm even friends with the guy. Sometimes he can be an absolute ass, and it's hard to remember why we're even friends at all. Honestly, I think we're only friends because we're in the same school and on the same team.

My mom greets me from the living room when I get back home that night. She usually works until seven or eight, so she doesn't get to attend many of the games.

"How was the game?" she asks.

"It was good. We won."

"That's great." She smiles at me. "Hopefully, I can make your next home game."

"Yeah, that'd be cool. Hey, I'm gonna go to bed."

"Okay, g'night, honey."

"Night, Ma."

Lying in bed, my usual nightly habit is scrolling through Instagram or Twitter. But tonight, I'm anxious. Even though I sent the last text, telling her I had to go for a bit, I wonder if she texted me back. Or maybe sometime during the game.

Turning on my phone, I see no new alerts and frown a little. But we did talk a lot during that hour earlier. I wonder if I should send her a text. Is it too late? Would she be asleep? Why would I text her this late? What would we talk about? I close my eyes, letting out a long sigh. I can't believe I'm acting like this over a girl I haven't even met.

BigBaller27: You awake?

I drop the phone to my chest, wondering if she's asleep

or if she'll reply. Closing my eyes, I try to calm my nerves. Even if she's sleeping, she'll still see the text in the morning.

Emerald22: Yes :)

I know I shouldn't read anything into it, but she added a smiley face. She could've typed yes and waited for my response, but she didn't.

BigBaller27: I'm about to go to sleep.
Emerald22: Oh, ok.
BigBaller27: Just wanted to say goodnight :)

My chest tightens as I wait for a reply. Was that too much? Was it too soon? It's like a first kiss, I guess. You don't want to try and make out with the girl the first time you guys talk, but what if you wait too long? Then you lend yourself over to possibly being in the friend zone. What am I saying, friend zone? She technically isn't even my friend. She's a texting buddy. But still ... there's something about the way we've texted so far.

Emerald22: Thx. Sweet dreams ;)

Chapter 10

Emma

The moment my eyes open I reach for my phone. A small frown curves over my lips, as I see no new texts. Then I remember about last night and smile. He texted me to say goodnight. It was the sweetest thing ever! There was a small part of me nervous about telling him sweet dreams, but only a little. I debated with myself right after I sent it, thinking it might've been a little much, but he initiated the goodnight. Sweet dreams was a proper response.

The smile doesn't leave my face the entire morning. When I get into Jen's car, she looks at me confused, sipping a Frappuccino.

"Wow, what's got you all frenetic?"

My eyes dart over to her, as she hands me a drink she got me. The smile's still on my lips as I sip my mocha frapp'. Opening my text messages, I show her the screen.

"He texted me last night to say goodnight."

Jen's mouth drops open as she grabs my phone and stares at it. "Oh, that is too cute!" She starts scrolling through my messages. "Holy hell, Emma. How much did you text yesterday?"

"I know." I take my phone back. "We messaged each other for, like, a whole hour, before he had to go do something. We kind of set up some ground rules for our ..." I look at my phone, debating on the right word. "Situation."

"Ground rules, huh?" She takes another sip of her drink and pulls out onto the road. "Explain."

I go over everything that we covered, and by the time we pull into the student parking lot, I'm almost bouncing up and down on her seat.

"Next time, I'm getting you decaf." She smirks at me.

My phone chimes.

BigBaller27: Morning ;)

My mouth drops and the warmth I was feeling yesterday as we exchanged messages is back, starting in my chest, spreading out through my entire body. Jen looks at me and then at my phone.

"A good night and a good morning text? Okay, if this guy is hot, then you better find out who he is stat!"

I giggle as I get out of the car and make my way to first period.

And that's how it goes for the rest of the week. I try to contain my excitement, but it's difficult. He'll text me a random, annoying thing one of his teachers did, and I'll laugh. I'll text him, asking what I should get for lunch, and he'll suggest something. That's how I find out we both like Pepsi.

As the week passes, I start to wonder more and more

who he is and what he looks like. Does he play sports, or is he all about studying? Is he overweight? Would I mind that? I shake my head whenever thoughts like those start entering my brain because the more time passes, the more I realize, I'm starting to like this guy. And like him for who he is on the inside, learning about his likes and dislikes. Not some outer, physical appearance. This isn't a typical, high school relationship forming, where the homecoming king is dating the popular cheerleader girl. This is something more. Something real.

BigBaller27: U know, if we knew each other, I'd invite you to a beach party I'm getting dragged to this weekend.

I'm blushing brighter than a tomato for two reasons. First, he's talking about inviting me out somewhere. Like a date. Like an actual, real-life date. I hadn't thought about something like that since my epic-fail of being able to put words together with Paxton. But secondly, and more distressingly, I believe, is that he's throwing it out there. Meeting. I wasn't sure if he'd bring it up again, when I freaked out the first time, and remembering how I reacted is not helping anything. It's not exactly like he's bringing it up again, so maybe he didn't even mean anything by it, or perhaps he's just, like, trying to feel the waters out, or maybe he's just ... *Breathe. Just, breathe, Emma.*

I put my phone in my pocket and stare at my sandwich.

"Okay, that's it," Lana says, eyeing me suspiciously.

"What?" My eyes shoot up to her.

"You've been acting funny all week. What gives?"

I snort out a laugh as I look over at Jen, who just raises her eyebrows. "Nothing."

"Yeah, right," Micah says. "We noticed it Wednesday but

didn't say anything. And yesterday your eyes were glued to your phone for almost the entire lunch."

"No, they weren't."

"They kinda were," Jen says. My mouth hangs open at Jen in betrayal. "Emma, it's time."

"What's time?" Lana asks.

"No, Jen, it's not. It's only been a week."

"What's been a week?" Micah raises his voice.

"Nothing." I wrinkle my nose, looking down at my sandwich.

"Yes, something," Jen counters. "A lot can happen in a week. Hell, a lot *has* happened in a week."

"Are you guys gonna tell us what's going on?" Lana exasperates.

"Emma's got a boyfriend."

"What?" Lana and Micah both shout, almost both in the same high pitch.

"I do not."

"No?" She gives me an evil smirk. "Okay, I'm sorry. He's not your boyfriend. You just talk to him about everything, always exchanging texts and you tell each other goodnight and good morning."

"That sounds like boyfriend stuff to me." Lana eyes me.

"No, he's—" My words cut off.

I never thought about it the way Jen says it but is that what's happened? Has he become my boyfriend? How can a guy become your boyfriend if you don't even know his name? Or what he looks like? And if you haven't even kissed?

"No," I say again, trying to find my confidence. "He's not my boyfriend. We're just friends."

As if on cue, my phone chimes.

BigBaller27: Hey, no worries, though. OK? I was just thinking out loud. Or in this case, thru text ;P

Of course, he'd add that. I already freaked out on him once before. But even the small embarrassment of how I acted before, is soothed by warmth, as I read how he's trying to be considerate. He really does seem like a great guy.

"Is that him?" Lana asks this time more intrigue in her voice.

"Yes." I blush.

"Emma!" Micah smiles. "This is awesome. Who is he?"

"Yeah, Emma. Who is he?" Jen teases. Lana and Micah look at her strangely.

"Wait a second. Jen, you said it first. How do you not know who he is?"

Jen doesn't say anything. She just shoots a look at me, waiting for me to spill the beans. Micah and Lana's faces turn toward me, waiting for my response. I drop my head to the table in defeat.

"I don't actually know him," I mutter.

"Wait, what?" Micah says. "You don't know him?"

"You said you've been texting every day," Lana says.

"We have," I answer, my face still on the table. "But ... we don't know each other. I don't know his name, and he doesn't know mine."

"I don't understand." Micah drops his head onto his fist, staring at me.

"It's a long story." I finally look up at them, not wanting to go over it but everyone's eyes, including Jen's, are locked on me.

So, I explain what happened with the wrong number text message and how everything escalated from there. I go over the goodnight/good morning texts, and everything we've been texting about since. Well, not everything, but the highlights.

"Ooh." Lana swoons, wrapping her arms around one of Micah's. "This is so cute. It's like writing love letters or something. It's so romantic."

I'm finally able to release a smile, happy that Lana isn't freaking out about it. She genuinely seems excited for me. I'm not sure if it's because they know now, or I've given myself a chance to calm down, but I thought of the perfect reply to his text message. It'll have to wait though, so Lana can get our girl talk out of the way.

Before it starts, Micah turns and looks at Lana like she's growing a second head. "This is so weird."

Chapter 11

Carter

"Dude, that is so freaking weird," Matt says, as we walk to history class after lunch.

We went the entire week without him bringing up the subject of why I was acting weird at practice, probably because I've been in a great mood all week. I'd taken the chance on the goodnight text, and it worked out. The next morning, I decided to swing for the fences and text her good morning.

Ever since then we'd been texting each other every day, multiple times throughout the day. I'd learned stuff she likes, like art. Her favorite foods and band, which was another plus because we both love Empire of The Sun. She told me about this great family vacation she went on with her parents. I told her how I love basketball, and I've been to over a hundred Clippers games since I was little. How none of my classes are my favorite, but if I had to choose, then science would be my favorite subject. I can't deny that it's insane, but it feels like the best possible way to be insane.

I've thought about what she looks like, but the more we've talked, I'm beginning not to care. This girl is real. She's genuine and sweet. Then I had to go and screw it up about possibly meeting her again.

I know I want to tread lightly. After I brought up the idea of possibly asking her out the first time, it seemed like she freaked out. Maybe she didn't know what to say, or she had to ask her friend. I don't know, but it didn't seem like a good sign. After this entire week, I thought maybe we were past that. Maybe, just maybe, I should take a chance on bringing it up again. But I didn't want to freak her out.

So, I mentioned the beach party that Matt has been hounding me about. I immediately followed it up with telling her it was no big deal. I try to make it sound light-hearted and add a winky-smiley face. But the entire lunch period goes by, and I don't receive a text back. Now I'm over analyzing the whole thing, and Matt arches an eyebrow at me.

When the bell rings to get to class, I figure it's time to let the cat out of the bag. This way I'll have a finite amount of time to tell him. By the time class starts, he can't keep going on and on about how stupid it is. Because even if he is my best friend and a good guy, I know how crazy this thing sounds.

"Yeah, I know it's weird," I reply. "But, I'm telling you, it's ... weird, but in a good way."

"Weird in a good way?" He raises an eyebrow.

"Okay, just think about this for a second, Matt." I try to keep my voice down, so people passing by won't hear.

"Remember last year, when you went out with Pauline for a couple of weeks."

"Yeah."

"Okay, so remember in the beginning you were all crazy about her. You thought she was awesome."

"Totally." He scoffs. "Then she turned out to be a psycho, stalked my Instagram page and blew up my DMs."

"Exactly. Now, just think if you had gotten to know what she was really like before you made out with her at Jeremy's that night. If you'd learned that stuff first, then you wouldn't have ended up with a psycho chick stalking you for weeks."

"Yeah, I guess. But, dude, she was insanely hot."

"Yeah, and?"

"*And* you have no idea what this girl looks like. What she sounds like. Carter, you don't even know her name."

I let out an exasperated grunt, shaking my head. "I know, man. It's just ... it's different. I can feel it. She's unique."

"I guess," he mumbles. "Hey, what's the handle you went with?"

I chuckle. "Big Baller 27."

"Okay." He laughs. "That's not bad. But still, bro. This is so weird."

"I know, I know."

Right before we get to our classroom door, my phone chirps. I let out a nervous laugh, from both the anticipation of the text message and now Matt knowing what's going on.

Emerald22: Sounds like fun. Hope you have a good time. Send me a selfie :)

I can't help the grin that hit my lips. Looking at my phone, I can feel Matt's eyes on me, as he mutters, "Oh, God."

BigBaller27: Not until I get a selfie of u ;D

Switching my phone to silent, I walk into the class and find my desk in front of Matt's, just as the bell rings. Mrs. Yanick walks over to shut the door when Emma whisks into the room, squeezing by her.

"Ms. Sanchez, you know when the tardy bell rings."

"Yes, ma'am. Sorry. I got sidetracked for a moment."

"Very well. Take your seat," she says as Emma goes to her seat on the other side of the room.

I haven't spoken to her since she bumped into me, but we don't really talk as it is. She's an artsy girl, and Lucas has a major crush on her best friend, or at least it seems like that. One thing I do always notice about her is her clothes. Not only because what she wears shows off her curves, but it's always different. Like when she bumped into me. She was wearing all this dark stuff, but today is entirely the opposite. Her hair is pulled back, she has some nice capri pants on that hug her ass, and a shirt that shows just enough of her waist that makes you want to see more. She would fit in nicely with Sarah and the other cheerleaders, the way she's dressed today. Though, I'd guess she'd rather gouge out her eyeballs than hang out with the cheerleader girls.

She turns around to take her seat, and her eyes met mine. Suddenly I realize I'm staring at her chest and turn away quickly. *Shit.*

Through my peripheral, I can see she takes her seat, so I dare another glance, just to see if she's still looking my way. She is, and her eyes beam hatred at me. Matt must catch the eye line encounter happen because he nudges my shoulder, and I hear a chuckle out of him.

My mind starts to roam about my girl, wondering what

she looks like. *Damn, I'm thinking of her as my girl.* She probably isn't going to be at the beach, but what would she look
like out there? Would she be in a one-piece or a two-piece
bikini? I wonder if she has short or long hair. I try to shake
free from the thoughts, but they keep popping up for the
rest of the day.

Chapter 12

Emma

I'd be lying if I said I'm not disappointed for most of the weekend. It's been a week of texting back and forth but on Saturday, my friend ... texting friend ... boyfriend ... *Oh God, I don't even know what to call him*, told me he was going out of town for most of the weekend and wouldn't be back until Sunday evening when he was going to the beach party. Even though I replied with something casual, the question crossed my mind; should we finally meet?

I end up going to the mall with Jen, and we hit up the art supply store since I need some new paints and brushes. Lana decides to meet us at the mall, and of course, the topic comes back to Big Baller.

"Okay," she says as we walked into H&M. "I've been dying to know. Just how well do you know this guy? You clammed up pretty tight during lunch."

"Yeah, what was that about?" Jen asks, browsing through a clothing rack.

"He mentioned something about a beach party this weekend," I say, feeling more comfortable talking about it. "He said if he knew me, he'd invite me."

"Emma!" Jen shouts, making a couple of ladies across the store turn and stare at us. "He brought it up again. You need to figure this out quickly."

I roll my eyes at her, as Lana asks what she means.

"He already asked her out once. Like, not so much point blank, but he definitely put it on the table. And then Emma freaked out."

"I did not freak out." I scowl at her.

"Really? You seemed freaked out when you got to my car after school."

"Okay, I freaked out a little. But, I'll have you know, I didn't freak out this time. Well, maybe a little, but I answered by the end of lunch. I even asked for a selfie." I smile at what I consider a brash move, though I'm sure Jen would've asked for much more than that.

"Okay." She smiles and resumes looking at clothes. "That's not bad. What'd he say?"

"Not until I send him one." I want to sound happy about it, and I am. But just thinking about his answer, makes me wonder about just what I'm doing, and how long I'm going to keep this up. He seems kind and genuine, and he does seem to like me. If I want to try and have a real relationship, I have to meet him. And I don't want to wait too long because even if he seems nice right now, boys are boys, right? How long will he wait until he decides that whatever we're doing just isn't worth it? Trying to avoid the thought, I turn around and start rummaging through a rack of clearance items.

"Hey, you never answered my question though." Lana looks over at me.

"What question?"

"How well do you know him?"

"She should know him like the back of her hand, the number of texts they've been sending each other," Jen says, teasing me with a smile.

"Thanks." I shoot her an annoyed look. "Pretty well. I mean, we've covered all the essentials."

"His favorite food?" Lana asks.

"Spaghetti."

"Color?"

"Green."

"Favorite Band?"

"Empire of the Sun, which is mine too. How crazy is that?" I smile, remembering when we went over our favorite songs from them.

"What about secrets?" Lana lifts an eyebrow.

"What do you mean?"

"You guys message a lot, so you've got the surface stuff down. But have you told each other any secrets?" The way she sounds and looks when she says the word 'secret', is both flirty and roguish.

"I don't understand."

Jen walks over to me, draping her arm over my shoulder while looking at Lana. "Lan, this is Emma, remember? Our sweet little artist, who's never even–"

"Jen!" I shoot her an angry look.

I've kissed a boy before. Two, as a matter of fact. Because Sophomore year, Jen dared me to at a party she was having. So, I know she isn't going to say I've never kissed anyone before. That leaves two options. Either she'll say something that would genuinely make my face turn red with embarrassment because both Jen and Lana are much more experienced with boys then me, or she'll say I've never had a boyfriend before. Which is true, but not something I'd like publicly paraded around while I'm shopping.

As I stop her from embarrassing me, worry starts to fill up inside. What if I meet this guy and I'm horrible at dating? What if I'm awful at kissing, or just terrible at being a girlfriend?

"I don't mean a bad secret or anything like that," Lana explains. "I just mean, you know, you guys talk a lot. Once you get to that certain level of comfortableness, you'll confess things to one another. It doesn't have to be huge or life-changing. It's just, you know, something between you two."

I nod my head as I stare at the pants I'm holding, thinking over her words. We've shared a lot of stuff. Some of it was trivial, and other things were more meaningful. He told me his mom raised him and that it was really difficult when his grandmother died three years ago because that was the only other family he was close to. But it didn't seem like a secret. It was just the path our conversation went down.

As my mind wonders what I could confide in him with, I hear a cackle of laughs coming from the other side of the store and have to force myself not to gag. Sarah Donovan and her horde of cheerleader friends. I look over the rack of clothes and watch as they joke with each other, near the bikinis. Jen and Lana follow my eye line, and we all stare at them, eavesdropping on their conversation.

"Absolutely," one of them gushes, as Sarah holds up a bikini top over her shirt. "Sarah, you'll look freaking hot in that."

"Won't it be cold?" another of her friends adds.

"That's the point." Sarah looks at the bikini once more and then flings it over her arm. "Hopefully I get Carter to warm me up."

They all snicker and move to another table of clothes. I nod to Jen and Lana, and we leave the store.

"Oh, barf!" Jen says as we walk out. Then, in a high-pitched tone, doing a horrible Sarah imitation, she flails her arms in the air. "I want Carter Dixon to warm me up. And by that, I mean jump my bones. Like at homecoming!"

We all start laughing when I'm reminded of Carter in history class. "That skeez is always checking me out in history." Lana and Jen both exchange looks, then stare at me. "What?"

"Hate to break it to you, Emma, but a lot of guys check you out at school." Lana smirks.

"Especially, those days you like to get dressed up in your skirts." Jen lets out a purring sound and acts like she's clawing at me.

"Fine, whatever. But still, like, at least have some decency about it. Look at me when I'm not looking, like the other perverts in school."

"He is fine though," Jen says.

"Mmm hmm," Lana adds, catching us both off guard, as we look at her. "What? Micah's friends with Taylor. We've gone to a couple of their basketball games this year."

"So, what?" Jen wiggles her eyebrows, elbowing her in the side. "When Micah gets up to use the bathroom, you just fantasize about the varsity basketball team?"

Lana smiles, raising her chin in confidence. "Hey, just because I have my dinner, doesn't mean I can't look at the menu."

We all unleash a flurry of laughs again, making our way to another store. As we continue to window shop, I'm hit with an idea. Maybe something that will give me a firm yes or no on whether I should advance this and finally meet him, or just drop it all together. I think we need to share a secret.

Chapter 13

Carter

We have a basketball tournament over the weekend, so I tell Emerald my text messages will probably be sporadic. When she replied about sending her a selfie from the beach party, I wanted to say to her we should finally meet. But I don't know how to bring it up without making it seem weird. If she did freak out that last time I brought it up, I need to tread lightly.

The basketball tournament is in Bakersfield, and even though we win a game, we don't play very well. The only good thing about it is that since it's a tournament, it doesn't count against out win/loss record, so we still have a chance at making the playoffs. Most of us are bummed on the bus ride home, but that doesn't stop Jeremy from bringing up Tamara's beach party.

"Dude, I just want to go home."

"Don't be lame," Jeremy says as he munches on some

chips. "It's the perfect thing to get our mind off this lousy tournament."

I start to shake my head when Matt chimes in. "Yeah, come on. It's not like you got a girl waiting for you."

I narrow my eyes at him while he chuckles to himself.

Jeremy looks over at me. "I heard Sarah, and her friends are gonna be there."

"Ugh." I close my eyes, leaning back. "Have at it, bro, she's more than willing to hook up with anyone."

"And you would know." I want to argue but know I can't without revealing the truth. "They're gonna have a bonfire, Carter. Perfect lead to warming up the body."

"Come on, man," Matt says a little lower, leaning back in the seat next to me. "Who knows if you're even ever going to meet …" He shoots me a confused look. "Damn, what do you even call her?"

"Emerald," I whisper.

"You got her name? Sounds like a stripper name."

I let out a laugh. "No, man. It's her handle. Emerald22. I just call her Emerald."

"Fine." He lets out a sigh. "But seriously, if she hasn't brought up meeting you yet and it's already been a week, how long is this thing going to go on? You willing to date a girl through texting forever?"

It's not like I haven't thought about that. I have. But I'm still not sure what my answer is. If I knew who she was, then it might be different. I'd be able to see her and talk to her. As much as I love learning new things about her and learning who she is, how long can we go on just texting back and forth, not even exchanging names? Matt nudges my arm, handing me a bag of beef jerky.

"Okay," I answer. "Let's hit the party tonight. Just

promise to try and keep Sarah off my jock. Ever since homecoming, she's wanted to finish what we started."

"Hey, you never did answer me about why you guys never finished." I look at him confused. He knows the story and how we got interrupted. "No, I don't mean in the bathroom. I just mean, you know, in general?"

I stare at the seat in front of me, thinking about it for a second. I know Matt will get it, so I keep my voice low.

"Was it insanely hot? Yeah. But, dude, the day I asked her to the dance, she already wanted to hook up. Like, literally. She texted me that night. *I* was the one who said we should wait until we knew each other a little better. Not that I'm not down for a good time, but come on. It just made me wonder who the hell else she's hooked up with?"

A big reason Matt is my best friend is that we kind of think alike. Most guys would've been totally down to hook up with Sarah that first night. And hey, to each their own. But honestly, I've never been like that, despite the rumors I've embraced.

And the rumors were running rampant through Woodbridge. Everything from how many girls I've been with, to what classrooms we've hooked up in. After homecoming, they went ballistic. It's like one little spark at homecoming unleashed a raging inferno, and I did nothing to quell the flames. I liked that it helped boost my reputation as one of the most popular guys in school. Who cares if Matt and I are the only ones that know the truth. So what, if some people thought it made me a manwhore or some cocky douche. You can't make an omelet without breaking some eggs.

By the time we get back home, the sun is starting to go down. I'm still debating with myself about going to the beach party, but I told Matt I'd pick him up and don't want to hear him complain, so I throw on some shorts and a hoody. It'll probably be a little chilly on the beach, but with the bonfire, the hoodie should be good enough.

We pull into the parking lot and make our way down the sand; the bonfire is already blazing. There are a lot more people than I thought there would be, but I shouldn't be surprised. Tamara's not only popular with a lot of kids in our school, but she's also the type of girl who knows people everywhere. I scan the crowd, looking for a place to hang out when I spot Sarah with a couple of her friends. She's wearing tiny shorts and a pink zip-up hoodie. As soon as she starts to turn her head my direction, I look away, so we don't make eye contact.

"There's Lucas," Matt says, pointing over to him, Jeremy, and a few others who are tossing around a glowing football.

After throwing the ball around for a while, we end up back over with the large group. I hear whispers going around about beer that was supposed to show up, but I guess whoever was supposed to bring it either got caught or decided to flake because everyone's either drinking bottled water or soda.

There's a log set up near the fire, and I take a seat, as Matt goes to grab us a drink. That's when Sarah plops down next to me.

"Carter," she says in a high-pitched tone. "I've been looking for you."

I raise my eyebrows, staring at the fire. "Well, here I am."

I'm trying to not even make eye contact, but I can't help noticing her stand back up and unzip her hoodie. At first, I'm wondering why, because even next to the fire, the breeze over the beach has picked up a little. Then I see why. She ties the hoodie around her waist, and she's wearing a bright, lime green bikini top. She's definitely well endowed, but I know she's not usually that tan, so I'm guessing she went to a tanning salon recently. And as much as I want to look away to avoid any encouragement on her part, I can't. I am a guy, after all.

"I just got this." She motions to her top as she sits back down next to me. "You like it?"

Trying to regain my focus, I nod casually and look down at the sand. "Yeah, it's nice."

"OMG," she says, and I cringe. I never understood why some girls do that, abbreviate things as if we're talking through texts. The thought makes me think of Emerald, but Sarah continues. "It's so cold out tonight." She wraps her arms around herself but does it in a way that she's pushing her boobs out.

I know exactly what she's doing, so I can't resist the logical explanation that comes out. "Um, then put your hoodie back on."

She does that giggle that some girls do when they're trying to flirt and leans in closer to me. "Mm-mm." She shakes her head.

I know she's either about to make a move or waiting just long enough for me to, so relief floods through me as I see Matt walking back to us.

Sarah gives me an annoyed look, as I call him over.

"Here." Matt hands me a soda. "They're all out of water."

"Thanks." I pop it open and take a drink. Matt's eyes are darting between myself and Sarah, while I'm trying to avoid her.

"Where's mine?" Sarah looks at Matt.

"Uh ..." Matt gives her an unsure look.

"It's over there." I point to the cooler on the other side of the group.

I know it's rude and makes me sound like a dick, but she's giving me no other choice here.

Sarah plays it off, giggling again, then reaches for my soda. "I don't want a full one, just a sip."

I let her take it out of my hand, staring at her in annoyance. Again, she's playing the game, taking a drink of the soda in the most erotic way possible, letting out a moan, and then hands me back the can. My eyes narrow at her and I hear an uncomfortable cough come from Matt. But it's all a game. It's all fake. And realizing that, I know I need to just end it now.

"You drink everything like?"

"Just the stuff I like." She throws flirty eyes at me.

"Sarah, what is this? Look, I don't want to be rude, but I'm not into it, okay?"

Instantly, her demeanor changes. She straightens up and stares at me. "What?"

"Seriously." I wave around the crowd but keep my voice down. "There are a ton of guys here. Just go talk to one of them." Her mouth drops, before I add, "Sorry."

I look over at Matt, who's half amazed and half in horror. Sarah stands up, zipping her hoodie back up. "You're an asshole."

I should just let her go and ignore it. But the fact that she's mad at me after *she's* been the annoying one this entire time pulls at me.

"Yeah. But I'm an asshole you gave a handjob to. Have a nice night."

The appalled look on her face morphs into pure hatred. "Fuck you."

"Oh, my God, dude," Matt whispers as she storms away, trying to contain his laughter. "That was unbelievable."

I just look back at the fire, not feeling good about any of it. I wish I hadn't said it, even if it is true. I wish I could've just been friendly, or at least courteous. I think of Emerald and how she seems so sweet. If she didn't like someone, she probably wouldn't try to embarrass them.

"I'm gonna take a walk," I say, getting up and leaving Matt behind.

As I get further away from the crowd, I pull out my phone and scan the recent text messages I've sent. Maybe tonight's the night I should just put it all out there. Tell her I want to meet and find out just what the hell this thing is between us. Before I can type anything, my phone chirps.

Emerald22: #SecretSunday

I smile, as I reply.

BigBaller27: What does that mean?
Emerald22: Tell me something
Emerald22: Tell me something no one else knows :)

I bite the inside of my lip. This is interesting. But what can I say? I don't have any secrets that Matt doesn't already know.

BigBaller27: My best friend knows most of my secrets
Emerald22: Yeah, so does mine :/
Emerald: Okay, something only your best friend
would know ;)

My first thought is about Sarah since it just happened. I think about telling her that I'm looked at as a player, with all this experience, but it's all fake. I decide not to though. First of all, that just makes me sound like a douche. And secondly, what if she really does have experience. That'd be a little embarrassing. Then I remember something else I think about from time to time, even though I try not to. Something only Matt knows.

BigBaller27: Okay...
BigBaller27: Everyone knows it's just my mom and me. That my dad left when I was little.
BigBaller27: What most people don't know, is it's because I walked in on him having sex with my babysitter when I was five. I was little and had no idea what was happening, so I told my mom. There was a huge argument that night and the next day he was gone. I haven't seen him since.

I stare down at my phone, nervous about hitting the send button. This is one of the most intimate details of my life I'm sharing with her. Letting out a breath, I hit send.

Chapter 14

Emma

Oh. My. God. I blink as I re-read the screen a few times. I'm instantly regretting thinking of this stupid game. Stupid Lana, with her stupid comment about sharing stupid secrets. It's not that I feel weird about him sharing something so private with me. It's the opposite. He's trusting me. He's sharing this part of his life with me, that almost no one else knows about. It's in that moment that I know I have to meet him. But first I should apologize.

Emerald22: Oh God, I'm so sorry
BigBaller27: It's no big deal. I mean, I guess it was at the time, but u know
Emerald22: No, it is a big deal. I feel horrible
BigBaller27: Don't. I don't mind sharing that with you :)
Plus, my mom is a great 'father' for me too
Emerald22: Thank u but I DO! I thought this would be a

fun little thing, but it got super serious. And I have liter-
ally nothing as serious as that
BigBaller27: Well that's a good thing
Emerald: No, I feel so stupid now. My secret is so dumb
and inconsequential compared to yours
BigBaller27: Secrets are secrets :) what's urs?

I bite my bottom lip as I type in my answer, feeling like
it's the lamest secret in the world now.

Emerald22: I have this tiny scar on the bottom of my
chin. You can't really see it anymore, especially if I'm
wearing make-up, but it's there. I got it when I was
seven after falling off my bike. It needed three stitches,
and all the boys made fun of me at school because of it
:/

I wait patiently for him to laugh at me. Laugh at my
horrible excuse of a secret, compared to the life-altering one
he shared with me. When he replies, most of my nerves
dissipate, and I smile.

BigBaller27: I would've beat up any boy who laughed
at you ;)

Butterflies.

Emerald22: We should meet.
BigBaller27: Yes!
BigBaller27: When?
BigBaller27: Where?
BigBaller27: Sorry, was that too quick of a reply? >//<

I let out a little laugh at his embarrassed emoji and excitement, which gets me excited.

Emerald22: How about tomorrow? During lunch?
BigBaller27: Absolutely. Where?

I don't want it to be in the cafeteria, with everyone around. In the quad could work, but then I'd have Jen, Micah, and Lana all looking over each other, waiting. Of course, I'll tell them who he is, but I want this to be private first. Just for us.

Emerald22: How about the courtyard, near the front of the school. There's that grassy area and that big oak tree?
BigBaller27: Perfect. How will I know who you are?

A smile creeps across my lips.

Emerald22: I'll be wearing my Hogwarts Hufflepuff shirt, sitting under the oak tree.
BigBaller27: Um, hufflepuff???
Emerald22: U know, from Harry Potter?
BigBaller27: I've only seen the movies, and it's been a while.
Emerald22: Ugh, you have so much to learn lol
BigBaller27: Can't wait for you to teach me ;D

I can't contain the smile on my face.

Emerald22: Fine. I'll be wearing a Star Wars shirt. Better?
BigBaller27: Now that I can recognize.
Emerald22: Okay :)
BigBaller27: Okay

The nerves are building up in my stomach, and suddenly I have no idea what to talk about.

Emerald22: So... I guess I'll see u tomorrow
BigBaller27: I guess you will ;)

It's just an emoji. I shouldn't read anything into it, but I can't help it. He was so excited by his response and ready to meet. And *I'm* ready to meet.

The night is restless, and I don't know how much sleep I get. It isn't much. Getting up in the morning, I throw on a pair of pants, my Chucks, and my Star Wars shirt. I can't contain the bounce in my step as I make my way out to Jen when she picks me up.

"Holy crap." Jen looks at me grinning. "You look like it's Christmas morning."

"It's gonna be a good day."

"And why is that?" she asks, starting to drive.

"Oh, you know, the sun's out. I think I know what I'm painting for the art show. And ..." I pause to glance over at her and wait till she looks back at me.

"Yeah, and?"

"I'm meeting him today!" I let out a high-pitched scream, and Jen's mouth drops open for a second before she starts screaming with me.

"Ohmygodohmygodohmygod!"

"I know!" We can't contain the laughter that starts between us.

"When?"

"Today at lunch."

"Oh, I'm so gonna be spying on you!"

"No, Jen," I say, but can't keep the smile off my face. "I want to meet him privately first."

"But I want to know who it is!" She pouts.

"You will, but I want to meet him alone first. This is ... I don't know. This is special."

"What if he takes a friend?"

"He won't."

"How do you know? Did you ask him?"

"No, but I know he won't. I know him. I'm sure he wants it to be just as special."

"Oh, God." She rolls her eyes. "Fine. But you better text me as soon as you two are done swooning into each other's eyes."

I nod to her but keep smiling as I look out through the window.

The entire day seems to drag. First period, second period, and so on. By fourth period, the class right before lunch, I seriously think time is standing still. I don't even remember what my teacher is talking about, as every two minutes my eyes jump to the clock on the wall, doing everything I can to will the time to move faster.

When the bell rings for lunch, every butterfly in the world seems to be residing in my stomach. My fingers tighten around the straps of my backpack as I make my way to the oak tree. Not many students eat their lunch in the courtyard, and as I get there, I'm relieved to see only a few kids sitting in the area.

Sitting under the tree, I begin to over-think how I should be sitting. Legs crossed? Legs under me? Maybe I shouldn't be sitting, and just be standing up waiting for him. Trying to calm myself down, I pull out my sketchbook and aimlessly start drawing.

Chapter 15

Carter

"I can't believe you're doing this," Matt mutters next to me as we walk down the hall.

I told him about it this morning when I saw him, and he seemed just as nervous as me.

"I know." I glance around as we stop at the end of the hall. "Okay, bro. This is where I leave you."

"Man." He curls his lip. "I can't believe you're not even telling me where you're meeting her."

"Dude, if this girl is even a tenth of a percent as real as she's been acting, I don't want to screw this up. Besides, you're gonna see me right after lunch."

"All right, fine." He raises a fist, and I hit his knuckles. "Good luck."

"Thanks."

Looking behind me to double check and make sure he's leaving, I watch him turn a corner, then I turn around and head towards the courtyard of the school. As I get there, I peek around. There are a few people eating lunch, a couple off to the side, but for the most part, it's pretty empty. Over to the left sits the large oak tree. A bowling ball of nerves abruptly drops in my stomach. My feet freeze. I mentally roll up my sleeves and force them to move. This is happening.

As I get closer, I can see someone sitting behind the tree. An arm moves, and it looks like a girl's. Then she flips over a piece of paper.

Instead of going straight towards the tree, I walk to the side. I have to see this girl first to see if I know her. As I take a few more steps, she comes into focus, and my mouth drops open. I can't believe it. Sketching in a notebook, wearing a black *Star Wars* shirt, is Emma Sanchez. The same *Star Wars* shirt she was wearing when she bumped into me last week.

I do a double take. Then a triple take. No way. No-freaking-way. My mystery girl is Emma Sanchez. How in the world is this happening? I stay off in the distance a few more minutes, just watching her and trying to piece everything together, but there's nothing to piece together. It isn't some grand scheme. I texted the wrong number, which evidently was hers. She looks as pretty as she always does and it seems like she curled her hair a little. She's wearing some short pants again, only these are black. I watch her as she studies her sketchbook, her fingers waving over the paper with a pencil.

Of course, she doesn't have a care in the world. She's real. She's probably the realest person I've ever known. And there she is waiting for a guy, me, but still enjoying her life.

I turn around and start to walk away, but I can't. Facing away from her, I peer over my shoulder just as she pulls out her cell phone. A small frown crosses her lips. She's waiting for him. For me. Damn it, what the hell did I do?

I can't just leave her. What kind of asshole would that make me? I know Sarah called me that last night, but she was mad that I didn't want to hook up with her. If I just bail on Emma, then I really am an asshole. A certified douchebag.

Facing her direction, every muscle in my body tenses. With every step I take, I get closer, and I have no freaking clue what to say. *Hey, Emma. Guess what? I'm BigBaller27!* Yeah right, she'll flip her shit and scream at me. Or run away. Or both. But I have to say something. I can't just stand her up.

I finally make it to the tree. She puts her phone away and goes back to sketching. I've moved so slowly because I'm nervous, she hasn't heard me. I lean against the tree and look down at her, seeing what she's drawing. It's a sketch of the courtyard, the fountain in the middle. There's a couple drawn off in the distance, and I look back up to see them still sitting there. It's loose but detailed at the same time. It's really good. Thinking of our messages, I remember she loves art class and painting. She said it probably brings her as much joy as I told her playing basketball brings me.

"Uh ... hey, what's up, Emma?" The words come out muffled.

Her head shoots up. At first, there's a hint of excitement and surprise. But it instantly vanishes as her eyes meet mine.

"Carter," she groans out, her eyes returning to her sketch-book. "What are you doing here?"

This is hopeless. She isn't even giving it the possibility that Big Baller is me. She hates me.

"Oh, I was ..." I look around, searching for a reason to give her. "I had to meet up with my coach."

"Okay, then." She waves me off. "Go talk to your coach."

Trying to think of something else to say, I look back down at her sketchbook. "Whatchya got there? Is that a sketch?"

"Ding, ding," she says, annoyed. "Looks like your problem-solving skills are as sharp as ever."

She doesn't hate me. She loathes me. "It's good."

"Whatever." She shakes her head. "What do you want, Carter?"

I stand there, blinking, unable to think of anything. As the seconds tick by, I know if I tell her who I am it'll be a complete disaster.

"Oh, what? Nothing."

"Good, then you can leave."

Chapter 16

Emma

What I thought was the most anticipated lunch of my entire life, was turning into a lousy dream. Where is he? It's been nearly ten minutes, and I haven't heard from him. I pulled out my sketchbook to try and distract myself when who shows up but Carter Dixon. Looking cocky, his light brown hair waves in the air. I don't know if he meant to sneak up on me or not, but he did. And now he's standing over me.

He's looking at me like he doesn't understand that I told him he could leave. I am waiting for someone after all. Not like I need to tell him that.

"You do understand English, right?"

"Um, what?"

I look back up at him. "I guess not. You said you had to meet your coach, and that you're doing 'nothing' here, so you can leave. You know, put one foot in front of the other and walk away?"

"Oh." He looks down at his feet with an embarrassed look.

I pull out my phone and frown at the time. Fifteen minutes. Where is he?

"You waiting for a friend?" he asks, watching me put my phone away.

"No. It's none of your business."

"I know." He shrugs, still leaning against the tree.

"Don't you have friends to go eat your lunch with? Or maybe some more cheerleaders to hook up with?"

I look up and see a stunned expression. It's not like I know what he does, but the rumors are out there. Everyone knows he hooked up with Sarah at homecoming, and ever since then, the rumors have spread further, with multiple names. But he seems hurt. His pained expression makes me look away, down at my sketchbook.

I'm not sure if he's trying to change the subject, but he motions toward my drawing with his leg. "That's really good."

"I didn't ask," I answer, feeling guilty about the malice in my voice.

I can't help it. Carter is one of the most popular seniors in our class, who seemingly gets whatever he wants by flashing that smile. His basketball buddy, Jeremy, is disgusting. And sure, Matt seemed like a nice guy, but for all I know he's just as bad. Being the senior class president, I've heard a couple of girls call him President McHottie. With a nickname like that, I'm sure he has the same size ego as Carter.

But the thing that irks me the most is catching him checking me out from time to time. Not that it isn't a little flattering to know I catch a guy's attention, especially someone like Carter, but still. I may not be able to see them if they're checking out my butt, but at least *try* to avert your gaze if you're looking at my chest.

"Are you drawing that for a friend?" he asks.

Letting out an aggravated sigh, I close the sketchbook. "It doesn't matter what I'm drawing, or if I'm drawing it for someone. But I *am* waiting for someone, so if you don't mind please, it'd be great if you just move along."

The hurt that flashed before is gone, replaced by a coy smile. "He must be special."

The audacity of this guy. I mean, I know who I'm waiting for, but he doesn't. I could be waiting for Jen or another friend who's a girl. Or I could be gay. He doesn't know.

"Who said it was a 'he'?"

His eyes pop open, and I can't help the small smile that slips my lips. "Oh ... she?"

I shake my head, looking at the ground. "Not that it's any of your business, but no. Not she. It's a he. Now, would you please get out of here."

He rolls his eyes with a smile but doesn't move his feet. "Wow, he's gonna have his hands full."

"Oh my God." I fold my arms across my chest. "You are such a jerk, you know that?"

There's silence for a moment as I sit there. He mumbles something that sounds like sorry, but I can't understand it. Plus, why would he act all hurt?

"What?"

"I said, I'm sorry." Again, the candid look crosses his face.

"Why? For not leaving?"

"Jeez, I'm trying to be the better person here, Emma." He sounds exasperated and shoves his hands in his pockets.

I scoff. "Better person? That's a laugh. You're just a dumb jock."

"Well, I have the best grade in our history class, and I have a 3.95 GPA this year. So, no, I'm not dumb."

My eyes shoot up to meet his, a sudden honesty there. "You keep track of your GPA?"

"Yeah, well," he shrugs, looking away. "I'm trying to get straight A's this year."

I pull out my cell phone again. Twenty minutes. A small pit of despair starts to form in my stomach. Had he shown up, taken a look at me and walked away? Oh no! What if he showed up while been Carter's here and didn't want to interrupt us, thinking we're ... something.

"Carter." My voice comes out softer and vulnerable. "Please, can you just leave?"

Hoping against hope that he at least has a heart, I wait for his feet to move. They don't. "You must really like this guy."

"And why would you say that?"

"Well, I mean, you're insulting me like crazy, and you keep urging me to get the hell out of here. But lunch is half over."

"Exactly, so you need to leave."

"Yo!"

Someone yells, and my head spins around to see who it is. A guy runs across the courtyard, meeting up with his friends. My eyes find Carter's and he gives me a suspicious look. I can't keep the disappointment from spreading across my face.

"Guess that's not him."

"Carter, I'm starting to hate you more than I did before."

"You seem like a very hateful person." He chuckles.

"I'm not!" I argue, before letting out a sigh. "I don't need to explain myself to you."

"That's true, I guess." He lifts his shoulders and elation

jumps into my heart as I watch his feet move. He's finally going to leave. Then, as quickly as the excitement hits me, it zooms on by, giving me the middle finger, as Carter slumps down and sits next to me.

"What. Are. You. Doing?" My words come out slow, as I grind my teeth.

"Sitting," he says, before reaching into his pocket and pulling out what looks like a protein bar. He nods to me with a smile, unwrapping it and taking a bite.

"Uh, no. Absolutely not. You need to leave."

"Why?" He takes another bite, before looking around. "It doesn't look like anyone else is gonna show up."

The words sting. My face drops as I look around the courtyard. The couple that was sitting in front of me has left. There are a few other people, and they seem to be on their way out too. Tears prick the back of my eyes. No, I'm not going to cry in front of Carter Dixon. Besides, lunch isn't over yet. Maybe he got distracted, or detention or a teacher wanted to talk to him. It could be anything. But in my heart, the sad truth is starting to form. He isn't going to show.

As if sensing my discomfort, Carter gets to his feet.

"Sorry, I'll leave you alone."

His voice is soft. It's comforting. But it doesn't help the pain that's stabbing my heart.

Chapter 17

Carter

What did I do? I wanted to try and be charming or flirty. I wanted to try and make her laugh and then be all, 'Surprise, it's me!', but it completely backfired. The more time went by, the more she looked around, waiting for him—me—to show up. And the last comment did it.

I didn't mean to say it like a jerk. I was leading to something. I was going to say, 'It doesn't look like anyone is going to show up' and as she looked, I would say something. Anything. But it all went out the window as she looked around and I saw what looked like her heart break. Shatter. It looks like she's going to cry, and I feel like the biggest dickhead ever. How did I mess it up so bad?

I stare down at her in her derailed state. In class, even when she'd hurl death stares at me, she had this life about her. Vibrant. And thinking about it, that's how her messages come across. Even sitting here, in her defeated state, she's beautiful. I have to do something. I can't just let her sit here, thinking I stood her up.

"God," she snaps at me. "Stop staring me. You do it enough during history."

All thoughts of trying to cheer her up vanish as I look down at her, confused. "Excuse me?"

Putting her sketchbook in her bag, she stands up. "You heard me. Ogling at me like I'm a piece of meat. All you stupid guys do it. It's disgusting."

Okay, she's pissed off. That's understandable, but I don't want to be looped in with every guy in school. Guys like Jeremy, who actually did check out every girl's ass that walked by.

"Ogling? Really?"

"Yes, really."

She has every right to be annoyed. I know she's hurting and feeling stood up, but I can't stop the next words that come out. "Oh, and you don't think whoever you're waiting for—Mr. Perfect—isn't gonna want to ogle you?"

Her eyes met mine. "Maybe, but that's different."

"Are you serious? How?"

"It just is."

"Wait, so he can ogle you, but I can't ogle you?"

"Stop saying ogle." She puts a finger in my face.

She's inches away from my face. I see the tiny scar on her chin, almost like a cute dimple. And I can smell her. She smells like roses and some type of fruit. Is it a body spray? Perfume? As my eyes meet hers, she looks like she's going to tear my head off.

"Fine, he can check you out, but I can't?"

"Yes. Exactly."

"Why?"

"I told you, it's different. He's different. I know him."

A cocky smile crosses my lips. She does know me, more than almost anyone. Why can't she see that I'm standing right in front of her? Oh, that's right, because she hates me.

"You know him? How much?"

"It doesn't matter, okay?" She turns around and starts walking away. "He's nice."

Oh, that does it. I'm totally offended, in a confusing kind of way. I run in front of her, stopping her path. "I'm nice!"

"No, you're a douche. And a flirt. And a horndog." She stares at me as my jaw drops. "Oh, don't act all innocent. I know you and your friends. All the pop-jocks, getting whatever they want from the cheerleaders. Like at homecoming."

"You don't know anything about me."

"Yes, I do."

"Oh, really? Enlighten me." I fold my arms, waiting for her response.

She narrows her eyes, giving me a wicked smile. "Carter Dixon. Captain of the varsity basketball team. Every girl in school drools over you and you take full advantage of that like you did with Sarah Donovan at homecoming. Alicia Thompson loves giving the details of how you two hooked up over winter break. Oh, and Naomi Aguirre says she lost a pair of panties in the back seat of your car."

I just stare at her. I made out with Alicia that first weekend of winter break, but we never did anything more. I guess she liked to try and boost her rep too. And who the hell is Naomi Aguirre?

"You've probably been with at least a dozen girls this year, and it's disgusting. It doesn't matter how smart you are, Carter. Sleaze-balls like you are in every high school, every year, and yeah, girls are the same. But we're talking about you. It doesn't matter how many baskets you score. You'll still be a high school jock, just trying to get a piece of ass, probably not caring how many hearts get broken along the way. Oh," her finger presses into my chest as a lump of shame lodges in my throat, "and the way you check out girls needs some work. I always catch you looking at my tits."

"I ..." I try to speak but can't think of anything.

"Just because you look like you do, and have the talent you possess, doesn't mean you can get whatever you want."

She stands there, waiting for my reply, but I have none. There are literally no words. Most of what she said isn't true, but as far as my reputation goes, it is. And I'm the one that let it get to that. I thought it was cool. I thought it'd make me cool. The guys never seemed to mind. The girls didn't mind either. But to the one girl I cared about it did matter, and I have no way of defending myself. It hurts being called out for it, but not as much as knowing that's how she honestly feels about me. While texting I'm one person, a person she believes in and trusts in. But me, Carter, she's disgusted by.

She stares at me for a moment, reveling in the accomplishment of telling me off. I can't stand to be in front of her, knowing how she really feels about me.

"I ... I'm sorry I interrupted you."

Chapter 18

Emma

For all the timidity I usually possess and being shy around guys I like, if someone gets me mad I have no problem telling them off. To me, getting angry at someone is not the same as flirting with someone. Yes, they both bring out high emotions, but when you're mad at someone, the words come out easier. Like liquid venom. Not that I like being a bitch, but sometimes people just need to be told. I try to convince myself that Carter is one of those people, but he just stands there, looking more stunned and embarrassed than I think I've ever seen him look. A wave of regret washes over me. He looks hurt. No matter how pissed off I am, I shouldn't be taking it out on him. After all, it isn't him I'm mad at.

He turns to walk away, and I want to stop him, at least to say sorry. Yes, most of the things I said are true, as far as I know, but still. They were ruthless. But I don't stop him. I just watch him walk away, his shoulders slumped, and then turn around and lean against the tree. Now that he's gone, maybe *he* would show up. But I know he isn't going to. I wait the entire lunch period for no one to show.

I'm angry and hurt and embarrassed. I'm not feeling one specific emotion, but a torrential downpour of everything. I want to cry, feeling stood up, but I want to yell too. I want to scream at the top of my lungs but know doing that will just draw attention to myself. Who the hell is this guy? Why didn't he show up?

My phone chirps and a flicker of hope sparks before I check it to see that it's just Jen, wanting to know how it went. The first bell rings to get to our next class, and I text him. I have to know what happened.

Emerald22: Where r u? What happened?

I stare at my phone, anxiously waiting for a reply to come. I never take my eyes off it, as I make my way to history. No response. Turning a corner, I look up to see Carter and Matt standing by the door. It looks like Matt is trying to talk to him, but he's ignoring him and staring at me. A new wave of regret comes over me. His eyes meet mine, before he looks down, heading inside the classroom.

When I walk into the class, I glance over in his direction, but he isn't looking at me. His eyes are locked on his desk, his phone in his hands. He's probably tweeting about me being a royal pain.

I slump in my chair and pull out my phone again. I know he probably has his on silent, if he's even bothering to stay in contact with me, but I send him another text.

Emerald22: I don't understand...
Emerald22: Can you talk to me???

As Mrs. Yanick closes the door, I wait and watch my phone, switching it to silent. But there's no response. Putting it away, my face slumps into my hands, as I stare straight ahead. Trying to act like I'm paying attention, I do everything I can to not unload a downpour of tears.

When I get to art class, I should be excited. Ms. Hales had been speaking to me about our art show coming up, and she's very interested in the three pieces I'm preparing. For the next few weeks, we'll be working on them in class. I have a realism painting of a waterfall and an abstract painting, using our school colors. I planned on doing a self-portrait for my third, but as I wallow in misery, an idea hits me. I'll paint heartbreak. And it's going to be my largest piece, six feet tall and three feet wide. I start by adding the base to the canvas with nothing but shades of blue and gray.

When the bell rings to end the day, I have flecks of paint all over my arms, but don't bother to clean up. I even have it all over my shirt. It had been one of my favorite shirts, but now I hate it. It just reminds me of today's terrible experience.

As I trudge along, I make it to Jen's car; she's waiting for me inside.

"So?" she says in high-pitched excitement. But as I sit down, it finally all comes crashing out, and tears stream down my face. "Oh no! No, no, no. What happened?"

"He didn't show up."

"What?"

"He ..." I take a breath, trying to stop the tears, but there's no stopping them. "I was just there. Waiting. He never showed."

"Oh no, Emma." She reaches over and hugs me. "I'm sorry."

"I texted him, and he hasn't even replied. I don't get it." I look at her for answers.

"Boys are stupid jerks. You know this." She wipes away one of my tears. "He probably forgot or something. He's just an idiot."

"No. I think ... I think it's something else. I don't think he would've just stood me up."

"What do you think?"

"I don't know." I stare at my fingers, which are now nervously fiddling. "Maybe he did show up, and I didn't see him. Maybe he saw me and—"

"No. Don't even go there, Emma. He's an asshole. You're beautiful. Hell, you're hot. No, if he didn't show up, for whatever reason, then he's a worthless piece of crap."

A small chuckle comes out as I try sniffing my tears away. "Thanks."

"Come on." She starts the engine. "We're going to get chocolate."

"What?"

"We're going to Patties, over on Fifth Avenue. That cake place? Chocolate always helps."

I shoot her a weary look, before looking out the window. Somewhere, in the mass of students leaving campus, he's there. Why didn't he show up? What happened?

"Okay," I mutter as she drives away.

The chocolate does help a little, but the hangover of being stood up is still there the next day. I grab my phone in the morning, hoping for some sort of reply or answer. But when my phone shows no new messages, the hurt comes back. This time it's accompanied by anger.

I try to go along with my usual routine, but I'm constantly checking my phone. Endlessly thinking my leg is vibrating, pulling out my cell, only to find no new texts. Lunchtime is a little awkward, as Lana and Micah join us. It's obvious Jen told them, and they have no idea what to say.

"Okay, let's get it over with," I say, taking out my lunch.

"I'm going first," Micah says, seeming more alert now that I broke the silence. "Once we find out who this guy is, I'm kicking his ass."

He looks as hurt and pissed off as I feel. "Thanks."

Lana reaches over, holding my hand. "And then, once he's done kicking his ass, I'm going to kick him in the nuts until they fall off."

I have to laugh. I love my friends. "Seriously, guys, I'm okay."

"Yes, chocolate cures all," Jen says proudly.

"That's just so lame! Ugh, stupid boys!" Lana shouts.

"Hey." Micah nudges her, making her wrap her arms around him.

"Except you, baby," she says before taking a drink. "Oh man, look over there."

Jen and I turn to see Carter, Lucas, and a couple of their friends walk by. For a minute, I think Carter shoots me a look, but then he resumes talking to his friends.

"Rumor has it Carter Dixon's got love bugs."

"Ew." I look at her. "What?"

"Crabs. Sarah Donovan was telling people yesterday. She's not sure, I guess she's going to the doctors today, but she's saying Carter gave them to her."

"That's disgusting."

Suddenly I feel a little better about what I said yesterday.

I still haven't told Jen about talking to him, but I guess there isn't anything to say. I don't know if he was trying to hit on me or what, but I told him off. He deserved it. At least, that's what I keep telling myself, remembering the pained expression on his face as he walked away.

Chapter 19

Carter

There's no easy way of putting this. I feel like shit. No, I feel like the biggest piece of shit the world has ever seen. Not only did I manage to get a girl to tell me off, due to rumors I've been coveting for the past two years, but I managed to hurt the same girl. Effectively standing her up, even though I was there. I'm sure I broke her heart while at the same time, made her go psycho-killer. And I deserve it.

Matt's been begging for me to tell him what happened, but I can't bring myself to do it. The day it happened, we had a game, and to say I blew chunks would be an under-statement. I lost the ball multiple times, nearly fouled out of the game, and only shot two of fifteen. Out of fifteen shots, I made two. Two! And I missed all five three-pointers. I didn't even shower after the game, I just grabbed my stuff and went home. Oh yeah, we lost that game.

I know I'm going to see Emma and I have to try and get

back on track. I need to text her and apologize, but how do you apologize for screwing up that massively? I have no idea, which is why I haven't sent anything.

Lucas has to pick up some extra credit, so we walk with him to his class during lunch, and I see Emma, sitting in the quad with her friends. She doesn't look as devastated as yesterday, but she still seems down. Then they all turn around and stare in our direction, so I straighten up, hoping she doesn't see me looking at her. If she does, she'll probably accuse me of checking her out again.

And, of course, when I get to practice, things go from bad to worse for all the wrong reasons. I shoot poorly yet again, but I'm hoping I can find my rhythm before our next game because it's a big one. University High School and they're playing great this year. They're in our division, and if we beat them, we'll be in prime position to make the playoffs.

By the time we get to the lockers after practice, I get a few looks from some of the guys but brush it off. I know I sucked during the game yesterday, but we all have off-nights. I'm not sure what's going on, and then Jeremy walks over, giving me a weird look.

"Sup, Dixon? You feeling okay?"

"Uh, yeah." I shoot him a look and can swear his eyes flash down to where my towel is wrapped around my waist, before walking away.

"What the hell was that?" I mutter to myself.

Matt walks over to his locker next to mine and nudges my arm. I wait for him to say something, but he just stares at me. "What's up?"

He looks around the locker and then leans in close to whisper. "You clean?"

"What? Yeah, I just took a shower."

"No, man." His eyes dart around again. His whisper drops even lower. "I mean, *clean*. No dick rice going on?"

"What the? Who the hell said I have crabs?"

The words are louder then I mean them to be and Lucas speaks up behind me. "Dude, everyone's saying it."

"What the hell?" I look over at Lucas, who shrugs. Now everyone's attention in the locker room is on me. "No! I don't have fucking crabs. Who the hell said that?"

Jeremy walks over, pulling his T-shirt down. "I'll give you one guess. And if she does have them, she's blaming it on you because you dropped her ass at the bonfire."

"Shit." I knew Sarah was pissed that night, but I never thought she'd resort to starting rumors about me. At least, not those kinds of rumors.

"It's all good, bro." Jeremy smiles and I look at him like he's lost his mind. "We got your back. Anyone who asks, we'll just tell them you caught them from her."

"What the? No! I don't have them. Tell people *that*!"

He shrugs and walks away. Letting out a low grumble, I sit in front of my locker, while Matt looks on and the rest of the guys start leaving.

"You finally gonna tell me what happened yesterday?"

I take a long breath, staring aimlessly at the metal locker in front of me. I feel like the lowest piece of scum at the bottom of a five-gallon bucket filled with monkey crap. Yeah, it's that bad. So, now, not only did I hurt a girl I care about, but I also scorned another who is now spreading rumors about me. And not the kind of rumors I've grown fond of.

"Dude, I screwed up."

"How? I thought you were all psyched to meet that girl."

"I was, but ..." I let out a deep breath. "Damn it. Okay, you can't tell anyone this."

"Carter, come on." He gives me a look asking if I'm serious.

"I know, I know. But I'm just saying. Even if you had let it slip before that I liked a girl I didn't know, when I tell you this, it's going to freaking blow your mind. It blew my mind and then I screwed it all up."

"Okay." He nods with a concerned look.

"The girl? Emerald22? It's Emma Sanchez."

His face drops, stunned. "Are you shitting me?"

"No. And she hates my guts. Now with this stupid rumor out there, I have no clue what I'm going to do."

"Wait, hold up. Why does she hate you?"

"Because of what everyone thinks. What I've portrayed for the last two years of my life. That I'm some basketball-cool-kid that can get any girl he wants. She didn't even consider the possibility that I was there to meet her. She wanted to blow me off. She kept trying to get rid of me because she thinks I'm some Don Juan jock that's hooked up with every girl in school."

He chuckles.

"Matt, it's not funny. All those stupid rumors about me hooking up with girls, and that stupid homecoming bath-room one? She probably thinks I'm a walking STI."

The silence sits in the air for a moment. "What are you gonna do?"

"I have no clue."

Getting home that night, my mom left a note that she was working late, leaving twenty dollars for me to order a pizza. After placing the call, I sit at the dining room table, staring at my phone. I turn it on, stare at the last text she sent, then turn it off. The pizza place said it'd be forty-five minutes until it's delivered and when the bell rings I realize just how long I've been staring at my phone, trying to decide what to do.

Grabbing a slice and taking a bite, I sit down and turn my phone back on. Scrolling through our last set of messages, I see our #SecretSunday. I need to talk to her. Tell her how sorry I am.

BigBaller27: I royally screwed up. I don't blame you if you hate me :(

I sit there, staring at my phone, unsure if she'll even reply. Finishing my slice, I grab a second piece and just wait for my phone to go off. After the third slice, I figure she's probably so mad and hurt she'll never talk to me again. Then my phone chirps.

Emerald22: No biggie

No biggie? She's blowing me off. I did screw everything up.

BigBaller27: It might not have been for you, but it was for me. I'm soooo sorry. Seriously. I'm an asshole. I AM SO SO SORRY.
Emerald22: If it was such a big deal for you, y didn't u show?
Emerald22: Why have u ignored me for 2 days?

The pathetic ball of shame reappears in my throat. "Because I'm an idiot who you can't even stand to be around", I feel like writing. But I can't just come out and tell her who I am now. She's learned who I am. The real me. And I like that she knows me. I like that I know her. I have to figure out how to fix this and if I tell her who I am, there's no way in hell she'll ever speak to me again, in real life or through text.

BigBaller27: I wish I could explain, but I can't. I'd like to, someday, but right now, I can't
Emerald22: Do u have a gf? Is that what this is about?
BigBaller27: No, I swear. I...

I have to put it out there.

BigBaller27: I was hoping that was gonna be you
Emerald22: Ha! You've got a weird way of trying to show that
Emerald22: And that's a super pissed off "Ha!" btw, not some cutesy sarcasm thing

Even though she's still furious, just the way she explains how mad she is makes me smile. I have no idea if I can fix this, but it gives me a little spark of hope.

BigBaller27: I get it
Emerald22: Whatever

It's time to take a shot.

BigBaller27: I seriously don't blame u for hating me. And if u never want me to talk to u again, I'll accept that. And u don't have to forgive me because I'm not asking for that. I'm not even sure I deserve your forgiveness. But please, if u want to keep talking, I'm here.

I hit the send button, squeezing my eyes shut, and wait.

No reply. I stare at my phone until the screen turns off and then turn it back on. My message is still there, but nothing from her. Not even a 'typing' prompt.

Getting up from the table, I put the pizza box in the fridge and walked back over, turning my phone on. Still nothing. An hour goes by, and I have no idea if she's ever going to talk to me again. I finish up whatever homework I have, take a shower, and just lay in bed, constantly looking at my phone. Just waiting and wishing for it to go off.

Just before eleven o'clock, as I start to doze off, it chirps.

Emerald22: Ok

I let out a long sigh of relief. It's a short answer, nothing more. But she's keeping the door open. I just need an opening to try and fix this. To try and prove to her that I'm the guy she knows through messaging and not the douchebag she thinks she knows in real life. I have to do it because as I've been lying in bed wishing for that text message to come, I've realized a truth. I'm starting to fall for this girl.

Chapter 20

Emma

I should've done a whole lot more yelling when he texted me last night. At least, as much yelling as can be translated through text. And I *am* furious at him. But when I received that text, telling me how sorry he was, it seemed genuine. It seemed like he knew he messed up and he was ashamed. Why can't he just tell me why he didn't show up?

My mind races the entire night, trying to figure him out. I scroll through hundreds of messages between us, and he never came off as shallow. Or flakey. He seems genuine. So maybe something terrible happened, that caused him not to show up. Something that, even though we shared so much with each another, he doesn't feel like he can tell me.

I debate whether or not to even keep talking to him. My first thought is to text Jen, but I know exactly what she'll say. 'Hell. No.' And she's right. Why should I give this guy, who I don't know, a second chance? But the thing is, I do know him. At least, I feel like I do. So, responding with a simple 'Ok' before I go to bed, seems like the best way to go.

When I wake up, I figure if I'm going to keep talking to him, I won't bother telling Jen and the others. Why open that can of worms? Besides, who knows how this next round of texting will go. Eventually, I might think it isn't worth it and stop altogether. Remembering how everyone reacted, I can't stop myself from sending a text.

Emerald22: Btw, my friends hate u

I frown at the screen as it pops up. It might be a little too harsh. *No. He bailed on me. He acted like I didn't matter.* The text is justified.

I finish getting ready for school but never get a reply. By the time Jen and I arrive on campus, I think maybe the text was a little too much, but there's no way I can take it back now. Debating with myself on if I should have even sent it, my phone goes off.

BigBaller27: That's because they're good friends :/

Ugh, why can't he try to play it off or be smug about it? He has to try and be all understanding.

The rest of the day goes by without a message between us. I'm not exactly sure what to say. It feels like a fight, but I don't even know who he is. I don't even know if I want to keep talking to him, but something in the back of my mind says I should. I hate that part of my mind. I want to forget him. Cast him aside, delete all his text messages, and never think of him again. But, I can't. Everything we've talked about, everything we've told each other, then he just ditches me. Something doesn't add up, and I want to know what it is.

At lunch, Jen asks if he's texted me, so I tell her he did. That he apologized profusely and said he couldn't tell me what happened, but that he was sorry. Both her and Lana scoff at his apology and tell me not to text him anymore. I just nod.

When I get to history class, I remember about Carter and how I told him off. As I walk in, he's already sitting down. His eyes glance up to meet mine but quickly dart back to his desk. There's a tiny piece of me that wants to apologize for how I acted, but then I remember what Lana said. Who knows if the rumor's true or not, but that just proves my point.

After history, I finally start feeling more at ease. Getting to art, I walk over to my easel and pull out my giant 'Heartbreak' piece. Mixing some acrylics, I put the base colors down and begin to add purple rain with a dark cloud. I have an idea of what I'm going for, but unlike my other two pieces, which are straightforward—even for one being an abstract piece—I'm just feeling my way through this one. Letting my emotions guide the brush.

Ms. Hales walks up behind me as I add more gray to a dark red cloud. "This is interesting. I love the background texture you've worked up there."

"Thanks." I give a half smile while my hand keeps moving.

"What inspired this piece?"

I look at her, blinking. "What do you mean?"

"Well, I was looking forward to what you were going to do with the abstract piece. You've nearly finished it, right?" I nod. "This one though ... this is powerful. Do you have a name for it?"

I stare at her for a moment, unsure what to say. I know what *I'm* calling it, but I've only named it in my head. What would she say if I told her what it's called?

"Um, kinda."

She eyes me carefully, then looks back at the painting. "Well, I'm very interested to see where you take it."

That's why I like Ms. Hales. She's an artist herself, so she can sense when other artists are a little intimidated by something, and she doesn't push us. The next time she asks though, hopefully, I'll be ready to tell her the name.

Chapter 21

Carter

I cringe the moment I read Emma's text. Of course, her friends hate me. If someone did that to one of my friends, I'd hate them too. But I force myself to look on the bright side. She texted me in the morning. Even if it was to tell me her friends hated me, she still thought of me. Sure, not so much how I wanted to be thought of by her, but I'll take what I can get.

I keep racking my brain the entire day, trying to think of how I'm going to win her over. Even if she doesn't hate Texting Me, she dislikes him thoroughly. And me—Carter —well that's clear. She absolutely does hate me. To make this work I have to win her over on both fronts, but I have to make sure Carter is winning her over more.

Seeing her walk into history, I still don't know what I'm going to do. She looks over, and I avert my eyes so that I won't be 'checking her out' again. She takes her seat, and I just sit there, trying to think of something. I spend the entire class half paying attention and the other half thinking what I can do. I know I can't just walk up to her. I did that, and it was horrible. I have to find an opening.

When the bell rings, I start to put my book in my backpack and see her leave class. Walking out, she heads to the east wing, so I motion to Matt that I'll catch up with him and follow her from a distance. I know, creepy and a little stalkerish, but an idea is starting to form. She's going to the art building, so she probably has art for her last class. If that's the case, I can 'accidentally' run into her after school. I've already seen her sketchbook, maybe I can comment on that? There's only one way to find out.

When the bell rings at the end of class, I tell Matt to cover for me at practice in case I'm late and rush to the other end of campus, still unsure if this is a good idea or not. I'm not even sure if I'm going to time it right, but I'm hoping since it's her last class, and she likes art, it will take her a little more time than usual to leave.

Turning a corner, I watch as a few students leave the room. Gritting my teeth, I stay back for a minute, hoping I haven't already missed her. Then she walks out, and a bucket of nerves dumps into my stomach. Letting out a deep huff, I walk quickly to catch up with her.

"Hey, Emma," I try to say, but it comes out as a cough.

"Carter?"

"Uh, yeah." I rub the back of my neck, trying to shake the jitters, but failing miserably.

"Hey." She stares at me, waiting for me to reply.

"Hey. Um ..." I look around for something—anything— to talk about, completely forgetting my idea of mentioning her sketchbook. "So, um ..."

"You okay?" She lets out a chortle.

"Yeah."

She looks around and then back at me. "Did you need something or ...?"

"Oh, right." I snort at myself. Yeah, this is going great. "Sorry. Yeah, I just wanted to apologize. For the other day."

"What?"

"You know, for disturbing you, or whatever. I seemed to piss you off pretty bad, so, I'm sorry. I hope your friend made it better."

Stupid. Stupid. Stupid. Why did I mention that when she thinks I stood her up?

She frowns, looking at the ground. "He didn't show up."

"Oh."

She shoots me an annoyed look. "Don't say it like that."

"No." I shake my head, waving my hands. "Seriously, I didn't mean to say it ... however it sounded. Sorry." I suddenly have a new idea, but I have to tread lightly. "That's an ass move."

"Hey, I said——"

"No, I know. Sorry." I hold up my hands.

She still likes him. Me. Okay, that's a good sign. Now I just have to start changing the tracks to *me* me. I point at her arm, where I see spots of red and purple paint. "What's this?"

"Uh, paint."

"No, yeah. Right." I chuckle, trying not to sound too oblivious. "Of course, I know that's what it is. So, you just got out of art?"

"That's why there's paint on me, Carter."

"Right, yeah." Damn, this is going to be harder than I thought. "You know, you're really good."

"What?" She gives me a cautious leer.

"I saw your sketchbook, at lunch that day. It's good."

"Oh, thanks."

Okay, no sarcastic comment. I'll take that as a win. I have to get out of here quickly before I screw it up and she starts hating me again. "Okay, well, I gotta get to practice. But, yeah, I just wanted to apologize."

"Okay," she says, but it comes out low like she doesn't understand what's happening.

I give a half-grin and turn to leave, feeling like I finally did something right. Sure, I have a long way to go, but this is the first step. Now, I just can't screw it up along the way.

Chapter 22

Emma

The entire day goes by without any other texts. After school, and after the weird interaction with Carter, I almost decide to text Baller but then think better of it. He screwed this up. If he wants to keep talking, then *he's* going to have to make things better. But as nightfall comes around, I'm even second guessing that, still not receiving any texts.

When I get up the next day, I frown at my phone. But I surprise myself, realizing the frown isn't me being sad or even mad. I'm over it. Who does this guy think he is to make a big scene, well, at least a big digital scene, and go on and on about being sorry and still wanting to talk, but then I don't hear from him? Getting ready for school, I push it to the back of my mind.

Later on, I surprise myself again. Lunch starts and Jen walks up next to me, nudging my elbow.

"Hey." She smiles.

"Hey."

"Any more stupid apologies from you-know-who?"

"No." I shake my head, actually feeling okay.

"Good."

"Hey." Lana nods to us, as we sit down.

"Those glasses are so cute," Jen says.

"Thanks, I got them last night. Well, Micah got them for me, after we walked around the mall after the movie."

"Where is he?" I ask, looking around.

"He'll be here. He's finishing up a painting in art, for the show."

I nod and remember my paintings. I don't feel like painting Heartbreak today. Maybe I'll work on the waterfall piece or finish the abstract painting.

"Oh, did you guys hear?" Lana leans forward, lowering her voice. "Sarah Donovan is hooking up with Jeremy McCormick."

"Ew." Jen wrinkles her nose. "I guess she's like a basketball groupie, or what?"

"Hey, wait a second," I say. "Isn't he friends with Carter?"

"I'm sure she doesn't care," Lana answers. "And Jeremy is worse than Carter."

"No, what about what you said?" I lean closer, lowering my voice. "About the crabs thing?"

"It's not true," Micah says, appearing behind us.

"How do you know?" Lana eyes him suspiciously.

"Taylor." He looks back at her like she should've known already. "I was talking to him in English this morning. I guess Carter found about the rumor and went ballistic after practice." We all nod, listening to him. "Supposedly, and again, this is the rumor mill, but I guess she wanted to hook up again, at the bonfire. Well, Carter turned her down, and she got so pissed she decided to start the rumor."

"God, what a bitch," Jen says, before biting down on a chip. I look at her, a little confused she would be on Carter's side. "What? I mean, yeah, he's a manwhore, but for someone to spread rumors about you just because they won't hook up with you?"

"Yeah, I guess you're right." I nod and return to my sandwich.

"By the way, Emma," Micah says. "I saw that one piece you're working on, in Ms. Hales. The one with the clouds? That looks awesome."

"Thanks," I answer but can't bring myself to look at him. I've never liked it when people see my work before it's finished.

As lunch ends, I head to history and find myself thinking more about my interaction with Carter yesterday. He seemed genuine in his apology, even a little nice. And then he said he had to get to practice. That must've been some outburst he had when he found out about the rumor. He always comes off as this smooth player, but I can't imagine he wasn't hurt, at least a little. I know if that happened to me, I'd be mortified.

When I get to class, I figure the least I can do is be a little more cordial to him than I have been. Maybe even say hi. But as I get to my seat, I find his empty, along with the one behind it. He and Matt are both on the basketball team, and they miss afternoon classes occasionally.

Oh well, I shrug my shoulders, deciding it's probably for the best. I wouldn't want to yell at him again. Getting to art class, Ms. Hales pulls me aside into her office as the bell rings.

"Emma, how are you?" she asks, looking at some papers on her desk.

"I'm fine."

"Good." Her eyes met mine. "So, I was reviewing some scholarship information, and I thought of you."

"Oh."

"Yes. I know you've mentioned LCAD, and I've seen the pieces you've put in your portfolio." I nod, looking down at the ground. I think they're good, but this is my teacher. Maybe she has a different opinion. "And you know, Laguna is just as expensive as some of the other art schools out there."

"I know. That's why I'm applying for as many art scholarships as I can."

"Your pieces are excellent, and I happen to know someone on the board of the Woodbridge Arts Scholarship committee." My head pops up, my eyes a little wider. The scholarship is the largest one offered. Even if I don't get into LCAD, the scholarship can help a ton with any other college I go to. "I'm not saying it would get you it, but it might up your chances."

"Really?"

"Yes. But," she stands up and looks out the tiny window of her office, into the classroom, "I really think you shouldn't submit the portfolio until you have your piece done."

"Which one?" I look out of the window, towards my easel.

"The large one. The one that looks ..." She stops and glances at me. "The one that's full of emotion."

My cheeks burn. "You think I should put *that* in my portfolio?"

"I do." She smiles.

I'm not sure how to respond. I've drawn and painted personal pieces before. Things that speak to me, but this painting is so intimate. I'm literally calling it 'Heartbreak'.

It's my heart—my soul—on the canvas. Can I put something like that, something so close to me, in my portfolio?

"Well, think about it," she says as if reading my mind.

She walks back to the door, and I nod, walking out of the office and over to my easel. I pick up the waterfall painting I've been working on, I take a second look at Heartbreak, before putting the smaller piece on the easel. Grabbing my paints and brushes, I dip a brush into a marine color, and I'm just about to touch the canvas when I stop. Turning back around, I stare at Heartbreak.

I set the waterfall painting off to the side and grab the large canvas. I have to finish Heartbreak before I can do anything else.

Chapter 23

Carter

Jeremy leans over the aisle on our way back from the game. We were playing Mission Viejo High and doing well, until the fourth quarter. That's when it all fell apart, and they went on a 12-point run, that effectively ended the game. We couldn't catch up after that.

"Dude," he whispers, bumping my arm. "You know that shit's not true, right?"

"What are you talking about?"

I'm bummed about the game, but I've been thinking all day about how I'm going to fix things with Emma. After missing history today, I think I have a plan, now I just have to work out the logistics.

"You know," he says lower. "What Sarah's been saying."

I roll my eyes. "Yeah, I know. She's just on a rampage ever since the bonfire."

"Cool." He nods and begins to turn around. Then he stops and looks at me. "Hey, if I was interested ..."

I stare at him like he's a freak. A legitimate, mutated, abhorrent freak. "Are you serious?"

"What?" He shrugs. "You said at my party to have at it. I mean, I know you're annoyed with her, but, dude, she's hot."

"Yeah, and a psycho." He lifts his shoulder again, giving me a look that said he's dated plenty of psychos before. No doubt he has. "Yeah, whatever, man. I don't care." Then, just because it annoys me, I add, "If you like sloppy seconds."

He gives me the douchiest, cheese eating grin that only Jeremy can give. "When a girl's as hot as that, I'll take sloppy seconds all day. And all night." He wiggles his eyebrows.

A thought hits me - what if he does hook up with her? What if she tells him that we didn't do anything in that bathroom, except feel each other up and get our hands sticky. I push the thought from my mind, letting out an annoyed sigh. I'm done acting like some stupid player. That's what got me into this mess. Liking someone who hates me, because she thought I was some guy who hooked up with every girl in school.

"Hey, you got the assignment from Mr. Hilton, right?" Matt asks, sitting next to me.

"Yep."

"And from Mrs. Yanick? The history one that's due on Friday?"

I nod again, but this time I'm thinking about Emma. Before we left for the game, I picked up the assignment. I can probably finish it tonight or tomorrow and have it ready. But this is my in.

Maybe I can meet up with Emma before class and get her to help me with it. It's a long shot because first I'd have to tell her tomorrow after class. And meeting up at lunch right before class, what can we really get done, work-wise? She might see through it, but it's my only opening, so I have to take it.

The next day starts off great. I'm determined to make my plan work, but as the day goes on, I feel less and less confident about it. It's a stupid plan. Why would she meet me an hour before class to help me with homework? By the time lunch rolls around, an idea hits that might help. I can tell her I want her to double check my work. She's smart, so I want to make sure she thinks it's okay. Yeah, not a whole lot better, but it's something.

Getting to history, I watch her walk in. She's wearing this tight black skirt and high heels, that nearly sends me overboard the moment I see her. She always dresses so differently. No girl in school would wear something like that, at least not for school. It looks like something she would wear on a date. Or for a special occasion. But there she is, the skirt coming down to just above her knees, and her breasts peeking out just enough that it'd make any guy look. Then I remember she has art class next and my mind starts swimming in the gutter, imagining her getting paint all over herself.

Coughing, I straighten myself out and make sure she doesn't catch me looking. Matt must see what I'm looking at, as he kicks my chair behind me. I can hear him laughing.

When class ends I tell Matt to go ahead, then catch up to Emma, matching her stride.

"Hey, Emma."

She turns around, meeting my eyes, not as shocked to see me as the last time. "Hey, Carter."

"Hey." I clear my throat, determined to look straight ahead and not over at her, where her dress is pushing her boobs up. "Uh," I stammer. *Get it together, Carter.* "I was wondering if you could help me out with something."

"What?"

"Well, I missed class yesterday," I start to explain, finding my voice. "And Mrs. Yanick said there was that assignment due tomorrow."

"Yeah?"

"Well, see, I was hoping maybe you could help me with it."

She stops in her tracks, her head spinning around as her eyes met mine. "Excuse me?"

"No, I mean ..." I'm losing it. I have to make it sound better. "Not, help me with it. I can do it."

"Yeah, because I was gonna say, what was all that 3.95 GPA business?"

"Right." I let out an embarrassed chuckle. "Yeah, see? I can do it. But, I just want to double check my stuff. Remember, I'm trying to get straight A's?"

"Matt can't help you?" She starts walking again.

"Well, he could, but he's got a lot going on with Student Council." I crack a smile, hoping to alleviate the mood. "You know, President stuff and all that."

To my surprise, she smiles too. *Thank you, Matt, Mr. Class President.*

"Yeah, I guess so."

"Really? Awesome." I take a deep breath, trying to keep from getting too excited.

"What's your number? I can go over some stuff tonight if you want."

"Oh," I shoot her an apprehensive look. "Actually, can we meet up tomorrow? Like, at lunch?"

"At lunch? You want to go over your work an hour before class starts?"

"Yeah?"

This is it. I hold my breath as she stares at me for a moment, weighing the pros and cons, and whether or not she even believes me. I feel like my life's being held in the balance.

"Fine." She waves her hand in the air. "Where do you want to meet up?"

Before I know what I'm saying, I blurt out, "How about by that oak tree? That place I saw you sketching in the courtyard."

I close my eyes, realizing how dumb of an idea that is. She must hate that place. Even if she doesn't, why the hell would I bring it up? It's too close. She's going to figure it out, and then I'll be screwed.

"By the oak tree ..." she says, before gazing down at the ground. She seems hurt all over again.

"Or, in the quad, if you want? Or in the library. Wherever, really."

"No," she responds with renewed determination. "The oak tree is fine." She stops and puts a finger in my face, her eyes squinting. "Don't be late."

Chapter 24

Emma

Another day, another morning of no new texts. The last messages we exchanged were about my friends hating him, and now I'm wondering if those are going to be the last text messages we send to one another. But I went the entire day yesterday without a text from him, and more importantly, I didn't want to text him. Working on my Heartbreak painting has become a release.

The class before lunch I go over my history assignment. It's a packet covering different events of the Civil War. I went over the homework last night, and I'm not sure how much help I'm going to be for Carter. If he covers different topics than I did, I guess I can just see how good it looks. It still seems weird that he wants to meet up at lunch, right before class, but I'm trying not to think about it. It's not like he's trying to hit on me or anything, right? I mean, who would do that by asking someone to look over their homework?

When the bell rings for lunch I make my way over to the courtyard, and as I get to the oak tree, my phone chimes.

BigBaller27: Sorry I've been MIA lately. Been super busy

A revelation hits me.

Emerald22: It's fine

And it really is.

BigBaller27: How u been?
Emerald22: Ok
BigBaller27: So, just throwing this out there. Remember that time I offered to get u a soda?
Emerald22: Yes?
BigBaller27: Maybe today?

Is this guy for real? He bails on me, and now he wants to act like it's no big deal?

Emerald22: I actually can't talk right now. I'm meeting someone
BigBaller27: Meeting someone???
Emerald22: Just a friend... well, not really a friend. Just a guy from history class
BigBaller27: Should I be jealous?

I can't help the small grin I get, but still shake my head, because I feel like we're a long way from him being able to get jealous over me meeting someone.

Emerald22: U don't get to be jealous. Maybe if u would've met me like u said >:)
BigBaller27: Ouch

Okay, that might've been a little harsher than I meant it to be.

Emerald22: Sorry
BigBaller27: Don't be. I deserved that. Hey, I gotta go. I'll try to text u later
Emerald22: Ok

As much as I've wanted to exchange texts with him, I don't feel anything. No nerves from exchanging messages and no sadness as he cuts the messaging short. Maybe being stood up by him has affected me more than I think.

I take a seat at the oak tree, again not feeling anything. No remorse or heartache over remembering the last time I was here.

"Hey," Carter says, behind me.

"Hey."

"You like Pepsi?" He asks, and before I look up, I feel something cold against my arm. I look at the bottle, then up at him.

His brown hair sways in the light breeze. He's wearing his letterman's jacket, his name on the side of it, and his blue shirt underneath is just small enough that I can see his chest stretching the fabric. Handing the soda to me, his smile seems genuine, which make me stare at the dimple in his left cheek a little too long.

I shift my eyes back to the soda. "I do, actually. How'd you know?"

"Lucky guess." He shrugs and rubs the back of his neck.

I've seen him do that a few times now, mostly when he seems to get nervous, which confuses me. Why would he be worried about a soda?

"I mean, it was that or Coke. So, I had a fifty-fifty shot."

"Thanks." I pull out my history packet. "So, what'd you cover?"

He drops next to me, and I realize how close he's sitting. I never get flustered with Carter, but as I notice how close his knee is to mine, my breath catches. Clearing it, I take a sip, trying to re-focus on the homework we are going over and not that fact that my bare knee is gazing his jeans. I mean, that's silly, right?

"I covered the First Battle of the Bull Run."

"Really?" I ask, unimpressed.

"What?"

"Carter, that's the first major battle. You couldn't have picked something a little more intriguing."

"Sorry." He smiles, nudging me with his shoulder. I swallow a gulp of soda again to calm my anxiety.

Is it just because he's never actually flirted with me that I think he's doing it now? No, he can't be flirting.

"I had less time to work on it, so I wanted something I could cover well."

I read over his paper, and he asks to read over mine. I only have his word to go on about how smart he is, but as I read his report, it's excellent. Yes, the first battle of the Civil War is an easy topic to cover, since there's so much information on it, but his words are articulate. And even his handwriting is good, which I don't know why I notice, but I do. By the time we finish covering everything, the bell rings.

"Looks like we spent the whole lunch out here," Carter says. He gets up and extends his hand to me.

I look at it cautiously, almost like I'm a little girl and

think I'm going to get cooties. Then I think about that stupid rumor and how mad he apparently got. I don't want him to think I believe the rumors, so I calm myself down and grab his hand as he helps me up.

"Sorry, I probably kept you from your friends."

"It's okay." I pull my bag over my shoulder. "I see them every day."

"Cool." He looks down the hall, before smiling at me. "Well, we're going to the same class. Mind if I walk with you?"

"Sure."

As we walk to history, I'm acutely aware that I'm walking next to Carter Dixon. Not because I'm super nervous or have a few butterflies in my stomach. Where'd those things come from anyway? Not because he's captain of the basketball team or is one of the most widely known players in school. No, what makes me extremely aware of my situation are all the eyes quickly flashing our direction.

Carter must notice my apprehension because he nudges my shoulder. Again, a shot of adrenaline shoots through me. "You good?"

"Yeah." I nervously look around to see more eyes staring at us. "God, the rumors are gonna fly." I look over at him and see him look a little anxious. Then I remember the last rumor that was spread about him. "Oh, I'm sorry. I didn't mean anything."

"You heard about that one, huh?"

I don't have to see myself to know my cheeks are flush. "Yeah, but I also heard that it wasn't true."

"It's not." He nervously rubs the back of his neck again. "You know, a lot of stuff out there isn't true."

I scoff. "Yeah, but I'm sure a lot is." Carter gives me a hurt look. "Sorry. I guess I shouldn't be one to talk. You might be in the deep end of the rumor pool, but I've never even jumped in. I wouldn't know what it's like."

His hurt look is replaced with a smile. "That's a good thing. And I can't say I did anything to stop the rumors."

I nod, the silence drifting between us as we approach the door to our class. Opening the door, he waits for me to go in first. I walk to my seat and find myself looking over my shoulder, feeling like a total hypocrite, as I check out his butt before he takes his seat.

When the bell rings to end class, a light sigh of relief slips out, as I make my way to art. A welcomed distraction from Mystery Texter, but also from these new feelings for Carter? Feelings? No, they aren't feelings. They couldn't be. We just met up for lunch to review homework. That dimple in his left cheek is adorable though. *No, Emma.*

As class starts, I set up my canvas and stare at Heartbreak. Grabbing some greens, blues, and a magenta, I mix them around and start to add a lonely flower growing out of a brick below the dark cloud I painted. Getting lost in the painting, class is over before I know it, and Ms. Hales walks over to me just as the bell rings.

"Really excellent." She admires the painting and a sense of pride beams through me. "I meant to tell you earlier, but you're friends with Micah, right?" I nod. "I was hoping you two would head to the gym and get a layout for how we might set up the art gallery. Sorry, I know it's short notice."

"It's okay," I answer, putting away the painting. "Yeah, I can do that."

"Thank you. He's got the paperwork with the plans how I think it will look best, but if you guys think of anything that would make it better, just make a note of it."

"Okay."

"Thanks, Emma."

Heading over to the gym, I send a message to Jen.

Emma: Hey, I gotta meet Micah at the gym, to go over gallery stuff. Can you wait?
Jen: Sure. Actually, I'll meet you there.
Emma: U sure?
Jen: Absolutely. The varsity team is practicing. Hopefully, it's shirts vs skins ;P

I get to the gym but don't see Micah anywhere, as Jen walks over from the student parking lot.

"Sorry."

"No biggie. I'm super excited about your art show."

"Jen, it's not *my* art show. It's our classes."

"Yeah." She wraps her hands around my arm. "But your work is the only stuff I want to see."

I let out a giggle. "Don't let Micah hear that."

Walking inside, I'm hit front and center with the sight that Jen must have been talking about. I don't know much about sports, much less basketball. So, when Jen said 'shirts vs skins' I didn't give it a second thought. But taking up half the basketball court is a gaggle of guys. Half of them shirtless. Including Carter.

Our laughter echoes through the gym, along with the bouncing of a basketball that suddenly stops. All of them turn around, and my eyes stay locked on Carter. Basketball shorts dropping low with no shirt on. Like, shirtless. You know, his chest and abs not covered by any clothing. Whatsoever.

"I think you're drooling, Emma," Jen whispers, laughter in her voice.

"Shut up." I finally look away and can feel my face getting hot.

If the butterflies I felt earlier were just nerves of talking to someone I don't usually talk to, the colossal bowling ball of jitters jumping in my stomach is definitely from me checking him out.

"Emma! Jen!" Micah calls out and waves us over.

As we walk over, I can't resist looking over at Carter again. The sweat glistens off his face, and my eyes roam over his chest. I felt how firm it was the day I ran into him, but not those abs. Wow. His eyes met mine, and he flashes that single-dimple grin that I'm starting to like more and more, but it forces me to look away again.

"Yum," Jen whispers in my ear, and I giggle, even though I know I'm turning red.

Chapter 25

Carter

Damn. Damn in the best and worst possible way that the word could ever be imagined.

As the laughs hit the gym, everyone turns around. If there are cheerleaders in the gym while we practice, they usually have their own practice going on. When the echoing laughter of girls hit the air, we all stop and turn to see who it is. And there she is. Emma. Walking hand in hand with her friend and they're both looking over at us. Then my eyes meet hers, and it looks like she's blushing. Could Emma have feelings for me? Like, *me* me? Even if she did, I still have some ways to go to win her over, but our conversation while we walked to history seemed like a good first step.

I hold the ball, my eyes still watching her as she and her two friends look over an area of the gym. I know the guy is Micah but know him only in name only. The girl is Jennifer Harris, star drama student of Woodbridge. I'm pretty sure

Lucas has a major crush on her, though he never says anything. The only reason I know is because he seems to go catatonic whenever she's around.

Spinning the ball in my hands, I watch as they look at some papers Micah's holding. Emma is wearing little shorts with a light hoodie today, and those tan legs look amazing, even with little spots of paint on them. I can feel my face getting red, and I'm just about to turn away when a whistle blows—loudly—right in front of me.

"Yes, yes, it's girls!" Coach Hallinan screams. We turn around, trying to hide our embarrassment. "Which is why I told you guys its half-court press today. The art class is going over things for their art show coming up, so we're sticking to this side." He turns around. "Now, if you morons can remember how to bounce a ball, let's get back to it."

Matt walks over to me. "Well, well."

"Shut it."

He smiles and goes back to playing defense. Lucas and I are going over offensive plays and were assigned the skins team, which is why we don't have our jerseys on. Happy to try and take my mind of Emma, I can see him checking Jen out over my shoulder.

"What's the deal with you two, anyway? She seems to avoid you, but you can't keep your eyes off her. Why don't you just ask her out?"

"It's ... complicated." He lets the word hang there, trying not to look over at her, but his expression is pained. I don't want to push it, especially in the middle of practice around the guys, so I drop it.

"Today, gentleman!" Coach yells out and blows his whistle again.

Practice starts up again, and I do everything I can to forget Emma is standing behind me, but I can't. I can't forget it, which means I can't play. I physically can't. I'm losing the ball, slipping on the court, and I miss every shot I take.

By the time coach switches us up to defense, it's worse. Before, Emma and her friends were standing behind me. But now that I'm on defense, the offense has their backs to the girls, but I'm facing them, trying to defend the basket.

Coach blows his whistle again, and I see him cross his arms. "Come on, Dixon! Move your ass!"

I don't know if it's the sound of my name or the word ass, but I see Emma's head turns around. Jeremy's trying to take the ball to the hoop, so he's blocking my line of vision, but then I see her. Looking in my direction. I try to block Jeremy's path to the basket but don't plant my feet in time, and Jeremy knocks me down. Of course, Jeremy is known for charging too, so it could've been that. Either way, I grunt on the floor and see Emma flashing a small look of worry. I shoot a smile over at her, and she turns back around.

"What the hell?" Matt comes over, helping me up. His voice reaffirms that it was a charge on Jeremy's part.

"His feet weren't planted," Jeremy says.

"Bullshit," another player chimes in, grabbing my other arm to help me up.

"Ten laps!" Coach yells out and points to Jeremy, who grumbles before taking off around the court. I look back over to where Emma was and see her and her friends walking out of the gym.

"It's our last two weeks of the season, and if you bone-heads don't play tighter D, with no penalties, it doesn't matter how good we play. All right, ball up."

As we make our way to the locker room after practice, I hear someone arguing. Lucas and I are the last to enter, and I know it's not our coach. He usually leaves the locker room to ourselves, letting us keep each other in line.

"It wasn't a low blow; he wasn't paying attention." I hear Jeremy.

"Are you nuts?" I hear Matt's voice answer back, almost yelling. "What the hell's your problem? It's not gonna do us any good if our captain goes down with an injury."

"Whatever, Mr. President." Jeremy pushes past him, walking to his locker.

I shoot Matt a look, unsure what's going on, but he just shakes his head.

"You good, Dixon?" Jeremy asks, eyeing me carefully.

"Nothing a little ice won't help."

"See?" Jeremy looks over at Matt. "He's a big boy. You don't need to cuddle him. You guys probably do enough of that already."

I look at Matt confused, who looks like he's about to blow a gasket. Lucas also gives me a weird look.

"Where the hell did that come from?"

"My bad." He puts up his hands but has an expression that says he's far from sorry. "You were probably just scoping out those two chicks for something to remember later tonight. For your alone time."

"Hey, bitch." I step to him, and Matt gets in front of me.

Jeremy is not one to miss making fun of someone, no matter how crude or tasteless. And that goes for teammates as well. But there's something in his voice. Malice. As if he's trying to put me down somehow, which I don't get. It wouldn't piss me off as much, but he brought up Emma, even if he didn't do it by name.

"Oh." Jeremy's eyes go wide, knowing he's hit a nerve. "You were. Was it the blond one? You couldn't dribble the ball because you wanted to remember what her lips looked like."

"Jer!" Lucas yells, and I know it's because Jen's the blond one.

"What the hell, man?" I'm still in front of him, now with Matt, Lucas, and Franco between us. The rest of the team stands back, but everyone's watching. "What the hell's gotten into you."

"Ha! Me? Oh, yeah, that's great." He looks around the locker room, grinning and waving his hands at the guys. "You hear this asshat who's supposed to be our captain. Shit, I should've been captain, and we both know it. At least I'd be straight up with my team."

"What the hell are you talking about?"

"You know exactly what I'm talking about."

I look at Matt, who shakes his head, not having a clue. Neither do I. "We got a game tomorrow, so if you got some issue, you might as well lay it all out now."

"We're supposed to be able to trust you, Carter."

Still not having a clue what he's talking about, I look around the locker room. "What the? My handles sucked today, so what? And so what if I missed a few shots."

"Really?" Jeremy looks insulted. "You're gonna make me say it?"

Lucas looks at me suspiciously, as if I'm hiding something. But I have no clue what Jeremy is talking about.

"Say what?!"

"You're a liar, that's what."

"About what?"

"Guess who I hooked up with last night?"

My face drops. Now I know exactly why he's pissed. I look at Matt, who just raises his eyebrows. He only ever said it once, but he told me I should probably tell the guys that I didn't hook up with Sarah. That lying about it, even if I was just lying by omission, meant that if they found out, they'd either be mad or think I'm lame. All eyes in the locker room land on me. I'm about to get a first-hand lesson in rumors, fake or not, coming back around to bite you in the ass.

"Shit," I mumble.

"Yeah." Jeremy flashes a triumphant grin.

"What?" Lucas asks, his eyes floating back and forth between Jeremy and me.

Jeremy's in his element now. Acting like the big man on campus. I know it bothered him when I was named the captain, but seeing how he smugly looks around, I never realized just how much he hated not being known as captain of the team. Hell, not just the team, but all of us that hung around each other.

His smug expression hits me first before he looks around the locker room. "First off, in the vein of being *honest*, before I say this I want everyone to know Carter said it was cool. What were the words, Carter? 'Sloppy seconds'?"

"Jeremy." I shake my head. "It's not a big deal."

He looks at me like I just set someone on fire. "Not a big deal? You're captain, asshole. If you lied about that, what the hell else would you lie about? So, yeah. I hooked up with Sarah Donovan." Whispers hit the air, but I keep my eyes locked on him. "And guess what she had to say? Our captain here, Mr. Ladies' Man, ain't such a ladies' man."

"Jeremy," Matt says, urging him to stop.

He shoots Matt a look and then looks back at me. "Oh, well at least one person knew the truth."

"What the hell you talking about, McCormick?" Someone says behind me.

"Carter Dixon, Mr. Playboy of our senior class, is nothing but a liar. He never hooked up with Sarah at homecoming. They fingered each other a bit and then got caught."

"You're such an asshole," I mutter.

I'm not mad at the secret being let out, even if it is embarrassing. I'm more upset at Jeremy and how he's acting.

"So, tell us, Carter?" He flashes a cocky grin. "How much of what happened with Alicia Thompson is true? And how about Hillary Grayson? Oh, and what about—"

"Shut up, Jeremy!" Matt yells.

The silence fills the locker, and I take a long breath. Everyone's staring at me, and it's right now that I have a moment of clarity. Why the hell did I let the rumors take over my life? Why have I been so obsessed with wanting to be looked at as Mr. Cool? Who cares if I hooked up, had sex with, or even just made out with one girl or a dozen? What the hell did it mean? Nothing, in the grand scheme of things.

I stare back at Jeremy, his smug smile still in place. "Fine. You know what, you're right. I didn't bang Sarah at homecoming. Me and Hill just exchanged numbers. And all I did with Alicia was make out with her. Who the hell cares?"

"I do. Not only are you our captain, but you're also my friend."

I let out a loud, incredulous scoff. "Friend? Are shitting me? What kind of friend asks another friend if it's okay if they hook up with an ex?"

"She wasn't an ex. You didn't even have sex."

"It doesn't matter! I'd have never done that to you. Go after a girl you had just gone out with." A thought hits me. One I should ignore, but I don't. "Oh, and by the way, she was probably just hooking up with you to make me jealous."

"Fuck you. I could get any girl I want. Including those two you kept eyeing during practice."

And just like that, I snap. Even if he doesn't say her name, he's talking about Emma. About trying to get with her. I lose it and launch myself at him, my fist nailing the side of his cheek.

Before anyone can move, he throws a punch, hitting me under the left eye. A couple more punches are thrown before everyone swarms, getting between us. We both yell more expletives at one another, swinging wildly.

"Hey! Hey!" A whistle blows, followed by more shouting.

When the dust settles, Matt is standing in front of me, with Franco and a couple of others. Lucas is in front of Jeremy and the rest of the team. Between our two groups stands Coach Hallinan.

"What the hell is going on in here?"

"Nothing," Jeremy mutters, but Coach looks at me, making Jeremy give me an even angrier look.

"Yeah, nothing." I scowl back at him.

"Well, this better be the last *nothing* that I have to separate. Get your guys shit together by tomorrow, or else this nothing will turn into something. Like suspensions."

"Yes, sir," I mutter, still staring at Jeremy.

As everyone changes and starts leaving the locker room, I let everyone clear out before going. I catch a some of the glances from the guys, as I walk to the parking lot. Some are staring at me like I'm a liar, while others look at me like I'm pathetic. I feel like both. And I can only imagine what the rumors are going to be once we get back to school.

Chapter 26

Emma

As we go over the layout of how the gallery will be set up, Jen keeps making remarks about Carter, who she says keeps looking over at me. Then she goes on about Franco and how hot he is. Especially since he isn't wearing a jersey.

She also makes it a point to tell me she's already heard from three different people about rumors going around about Carter and me. Specifically, how Carter Dixon is now going out with the 'art girl', Emma. I try to tell her it's nothing, but she continues to give me suspicious looks, unsure if I'm being honest with her. I keep shushing her while we're in the gym, hoping none of the basketball players, especially Carter, hear her. Thankfully, Micah seems to be oblivious to all of it.

Jen's so sure I'm keeping the truth from her, she brings it up again after we go to the movies.

"Come on, Emma, spill the beans already," she whines, as we walk out of the theatre.

"Jen, there's nothing to spill. I told you in the gym; we walked to class after lunch."

"See, you said that," she says as we walk to a Starbucks next to the theatre. "But, I was thinking about that. You didn't tell us you were meeting him for lunch. And you spent the entire lunch together, going over homework? This is Carter we're talking about."

"I know who we're talking about. He's actually really smart. Did you know he's got nearly a 4.0 GPA?"

"Really? So, he's hot and smart. That's a plus." I roll my eyes as she laughs. "What? You can't tell me you didn't think that while going over *homework*." She makes air quotes with her fingers.

"Why is it so unbelievable that's all we were doing? Don't you think I'd tell you if it was something else."

"You would, and to be honest, I don't think it's unbelievable. Going over homework is such an Emma thing." She smirks. "But I saw him looking at us when we were in the gym. He was definitely checking you out."

She takes a step forward to the barista behind the counter, and I think back to lunch and the gym. Why in the world would Carter be checking me out? Yes, he seemed to be flirting a little during lunch, but it's Carter. That's what he does. Plus, it's not like I was dressed in anything special. Not like him, half-naked and sweaty—*No, Emma. Stop that.*

"And you weren't too subtle where your eyes were going either," she adds.

"What?" My voice is about three octaves higher than usual. I guess she did notice.

She steps out of the way, smiling at me while I order my drink. After I order, I make my way over to the table she's at.

"Hey, no judgments. I was checking him out too. But, Franco?" She closes her eyes, and I don't have to imagine very hard to know what she's thinking. "I always thought it's the football players that were fit. I should've figured basketball players look just as fine all hot and sweaty."

"Yeah." I giggle. "Must be the cardio."

I mean my comment in all sincerity, but of course, leave it to Jen to make an innuendo out of it. "Yeah, they must have some good stamina."

"Jen." I scoff at her when the barista calls our names and she goes to gets our drinks.

As she walks away, my phone goes off.

BigBaller27: How's ur weekend starting?
Emerald22: So far so good. Just went to the movies.
BigBaller27: Nice.

I'm not sure how or what to respond. Ever since the stand-up, we haven't texted very much. And when we have, it's been quick and not really in depth.

"Who's that?" Jen asks, setting my passion iced tea in front of me.

"Oh, no one." I switch my phone off.

Sitting in front of me, she gives me a suspicious look. "Emma?"

"What?"

"Did you get Carter's number?"

"Of course not." I look at her like she's crazy. "That wasn't Carter."

"Then who was it?"

"Jen, I don't need to tell you every single person that texts me."

"That's true, but you usually do. So, it begs the question; Who was that?"

"It's no one."

She gasps. "No way."

I clench my phone tightly. "What?"

"Emma, you cannot be serious. You are not texting that bastard still." I look down at my phone, defeated. "That guy is such a scumbag. Why would you text him still?"

"I don't know. He's nice, Jen. I know he didn't show up that day, but there's got to be more to the story than him just not showing up. There must be a reason. I want to know why."

"Then tell him to tell you."

"He already said he couldn't."

"That's lame. Give me your phone."

"No. Why?"

"Because I'll tell him to tell you what happened that day or he can go to hell."

"Yeah, I'm sure that would go over very well." She stares at me, holding out her hand. "What? Are you serious? No way."

"Emma, that's the only way this is going to end."

On the one hand, I believe her. And if this is nothing more than two friends, I do want to know. But on the other hand, if I come across super rude, then he might never text me again. Do I really want that to happen?

"Hold on." I hold up a finger and switch my phone back on.

Emerald22: Hey, my friend wants to talk to u

"What are you doing?" Jen asks.

"I'm letting him know that you're gonna be texting, not me."

BigBaller27: Ok???

I nervously stare at my phone as I hand it to her. Something devious and wicked comes across her face. It's almost like a smile, but at the same time, it's sinister. Jen's been my best friend for years, so I know how angry she can get if someone pisses her off. I also know the lengths she'll go to when she has someone's back. Her fingers work quickly, as she starts typing her message. Once she's done, I watch her reading over her message before she hits send.

"There." She hands the phone back to me. "I changed my mind. I just told him off."

I can't reach for it fast enough, wondering exactly what she wrote. My eyes pop open, and my mouth drops as I read it. I also can't help but feel a little warm inside, as her words that are full of malice for him are nothing but endearing towards me.

Emerald22: You've got some nerve! My bff is the best person ever! She's sweet and kind and a terrific person. I can't believe she's giving u another chance to even talk to her. I'm firmly against it. You're an asshole. Grade A! If u two ever do meet, be prepared for a swift kick to the nuts because I'll be spying on her and when she meets u, I'll be there. Jerks like u don't deserve someone as great as her. Peace out, bitch!

I want to laugh and cry at the same time, while she beams proudly. "Thanks," I whisper. Then my phone dings.

BigBaller27: Wow. I totally deserved that. Like I said, I can't tell u why I wasn't there, but I PROMISE, one day you'll know. For what it's worth, I KNOW ur a great person. And to have a friend as loyal as that also proves it. I know Emerald isn't your real name, but I imagine you're as precious as one and u have friends who protect you like a treasure. And yes, I am relieved and grateful and honored to get a second chance to even speak with u

It's the first meaningful text I've received since before the day we were supposed to meet, and even though I'm trying not to get emotional, I feel tears prick the back of my eyes. Jen sees my reaction and grabs my phone.

"Okay." She curls a lip, rolling her eyes. "As far as replies go, that one isn't bad."

I smile and take another sip of my drink.

Chapter 27

Carter

The weekend goes by excruciatingly slowly. After the fallout from practice, I receive a lovely text message from Emma's friend, who I'm sure is Jen. It's justified, of course, but getting hit in the face with the truth stings.

I didn't want to reply with some flippant comment. I screwed up and wanted her to know how sorry I felt. But admitting that was the exact game plan I was trying to avoid. I'm trying to get her to forget Baller and start thinking about Carter. So even though I don't want to send it, knowing it might make her fall for Texting Me again, I'm happy to be honest with her.

We have a game over the weekend and we tank. No, tank is putting it mildly. We implode.

Our team is more than divided. We're shattered. Almost everyone despises me for lying. The only ones that try to just play the game are Matt, Lucas, and Franco. And Lucas and Franco surprised me because they've been friends with Jeremy longer than anyone.

"Dude." Lucas came up to me right before the game. "That shit Jeremy pulled? It's stupid. I don't care who you're hooking up with or not hooking up with. I just want to play ball."

"Thanks."

But of course, that's the only bright spot. Jeremy took control, running the floor even though Lucas is our point guard. Jeremy called out the plays Coach called in, and every chance someone got they passed him the ball. By half-time, we're down twenty points and Coach is beside himself. It doesn't get any better in the second half, and we end up losing the game by thirty points.

Getting to the locker room, after the game, Coach Hallinan just looks around at all of us. He shakes his head, wanting to say something, but finding no words. You know when your parents tell you that they aren't mad, they're just disappointed, and somehow that makes it worse? That's how we all feel, as he walks out of the locker room without even a word.

Other than that, I hide in my room over the weekend, hoping I can avoid my mom and the black eye that's formed under my left eye. I do so successfully for the rest of Saturday, but on Sunday, I wake up and head out to the kitchen, looking for some for breakfast. Mom is already there, pouring some coffee.

"Good morning," she says, as she puts the pot back over the burner. "I'm headed to the office for some overtime, but I thought later we could—" she gasps as she turns around. "Carter, what happened?"

"What?" Still groggy, I don't know what she's talking

about. But as she stares at my face, I remember. "Oh, nothing."

"Did that happen at the game yesterday?"

"No," I answer, opening the fridge.

"Well?" Her voice is stern, and I know I'm not going to get away with not answering her.

"It happened at practice Friday."

"You got into a fight with a teammate?"

My mom and I usually keep a pretty open relationship. She knows most of the important stuff that's going on at school, and she knows Jeremy too. Explaining that he's the one that punched me means I'll have to explain the quagmire about all the rumors. We talk about a lot of stuff, but I don't make it a point to tell her what girls I like, make out with, or the rumors that go further than that.

"No," I lie. "I caught an elbow on the court."

She eyes me suspiciously, taking a sip of her coffee. Nodding, she examines my face a little closer, before going to the table.

"Okay, put some ice on it though."

"I will."

"So how are the games, anyway? I'm sorry I haven't been able to make it to any this season."

"It's okay." I finally grab a box of Pop-Tarts from the cupboard. "And the games, well, they could be better. We have to win our next two division games to make the playoffs. Not sure if it's gonna happen."

"You guys can do it. You were so close last year." I take a bite of the pastry, as I head back to my room. "Don't stay in bed all day," she calls out, and I mumble back to her that I won't. Of course, that's precisely what I do.

Monday rolls around, and I make sure to take a pair of sunglasses with me. I'll hear enough gasps from everyone during class, so I want to limit them as much as possible when I'm outside.

I still haven't texted Emma since Friday night. I don't know what to say to her. I want it to be casual, but how can I just be casual after the last thing I told her. I just want her to see me, Carter, and not start to like Baller again. Which leaves me with another problem. How the hell am I going to try and talk to her when I'm at school? I've already used the homework excuse, so what else can approach her with?

By the time lunch rolls around, I've forgotten about the fight. That is until it smacks me in the face.

"What are you doing, Dixon?" Jeremy says, as he gets to the lunch table I'm sitting at. I look up, see the bruise on his face, and three of our teammates standing with him.

"Eating lunch?"

"This table is reserved." He folds his arms across his chest.

"By who?"

"Friends who don't lie to one another."

"Seriously?"

"Yeah, I'm serious." They all just stand there, looking down at me, scowls on each of their faces.

"Forget this." I get up, grabbing my bag. "You know, you should've said this table is reserved for dickheads."

My words come out louder than I mean for them to, and a hush falls over nearby tables in the cafeteria. Eyes stay on me as I make my way out, Matt and Lucas walking over to me.

"Yo, where you going?" Matt says.

"Evidently, Jeremy got the lunch table in the divorce."

"What?" Lucas asks.

"I'll talk to you guys later." They each give me a confused look, as I turn around and continue walking.

I pass by the quad and look over where I see Emma sitting with her friends. There is a small urge to go over and talk to her, though I have no clue what to say. And since I have no clue, I decide I shouldn't and just keep walking. The only other place I can think of going is somewhere I know there won't be many people. And someplace that will still remind me of her.

Chapter 28

Emma

"That's not how art galleries work," Micah says to Lana, as she takes a drink of his soda.

They've been going back and forth since the start of lunch about the upcoming art show our class is holding on Friday. I plan on finishing both the waterfall piece and the abstract piece today, so all I need to worry about is finishing Heartbreak by the time the show rolls around.

"But it'd be perfect," Lana continues. "You all put up your pieces and then there's a model, or some hostess or something, and she points out what materials were used and how much the painting costs."

"Emma." Micah looks to me for help. "Would you please tell her?"

"Hey, maybe the whole traditional art gallery setting needs to be upgraded," I say, mostly joking, as Jen laughs.

"No," he groans. "We don't create art to be hocked like a

piece of jewelry or a car. It's called art for a reason. It has meaning. And purpose. If people want to buy it fine, but I'm not about to have you," he points a finger at Lana, "showing off my work, trying to be some saleswoman."

For the most part, I agree with Micah, though he is much more of an artist's artist than I am. He loves to create and find the beauty and meaning in the work of others. While I love looking at other people's work, I've never gone in depth in trying to understand their reasons or meaning behind their work. I just know my own. If people want to interpret my work, that's fine. But I don't like to try and decipher others.

"I think you're just jealous," Lana says, regaining her playful attitude.

"Of what?"

"You don't want your beautiful girlfriend to take all the attention away from your paintings."

"Yep, that's it." He smiles, rolling his eyes, but she plants a kiss on his cheek anyway.

As she pulls away, she nods to something behind us. "Look," she says in a loud whisper.

We all turn and see Carter walking down the hallway. I notice his sunglasses, something he doesn't usually wear. Jen nudges my side with an elbow, and when I turn to her, she wiggles her eyebrows. Trying to keep my cheeks from becoming red, I flash her a dirty look to stop.

"Did you guys hear?"

"You're the one who always gets the juicy bits before lunch," Jen says.

"Oh, my God." She seems a little flustered, so I know this must be a good rumor. "It's not just one. It's, like, multiple things. First off, I guess he and Jeremy got in a fight during practice." I look over at Jen. I remember Carter falling down, but there wasn't any pushing or shoving. "I guess their bromance is kaput. But then, everyone's saying half the team hates Carter now."

"What? Why?" Even though we only talked a little bit, I find myself feeling defensive of him.

"He lied to them all. I guess he was making up stories about hooking up with girls."

"Ew. What a sleaze," Jen says.

"That's not exactly true." Micah jumps in. "Brittany came up to Taylor in English and asked if it was true. She heard her name was being thrown around."

"And?" Lana looks at him.

"I guess Carter never hooked up with Sarah. Supposedly, he hasn't hooked up with half the girls people say he did."

"So, he just told everyone he did?" Jen asks.

"Well, no. Not exactly. He just let everyone think he did, without correcting them."

"That's one way to go about it." Jen laughs.

I should feel a little irritated. Or even annoyed with the news. But I've gotten to know Carter, and he seems decent enough. He's usually always with his friends, so watching him walk down the hall alone, a pang of sympathy hits me. I feel the urge to check on him. I mean, he was kind enough to come and apologize to me, even when I told him off. If all his friends do hate him now, he's probably feeling pretty bad.

I start to gather my stuff when Jen looks over at me. "Where are you going?"

In all honesty, I don't know, because I have no idea where Carter is headed. But I want to try and catch up with him.

"Nowhere." I look over, and she shoots me a look that says she knows. "Stop."

"What's going on?" Lana asks.

"Ask Micah," Jen says, giving him a smirk.

"Me?" He looks at her, then me, then at Lana. "How am I supposed to know?"

"You didn't notice anything kind of funny last week when we were in the gym?" Jen looks at Micah, who looks heedless. "Ugh, never mind. Text me before lunch ends," Jen says to me as I leave, knowing she's going to tell them my embarrassing story of checking Carter out during his practice.

I head the direction I saw him walking, but as I go further along, I can take two pathways. One leads to the courtyard and the other leads to the student parking lot. He could've gone to the parking lot, maybe to try and ditch the rest of the day. If that's the case, I won't make it there before he leaves. So, I head to the courtyard.

As usual, it's mostly empty when I get there. A few people are off to the side, sitting on one of the benches, eating their lunch. I see the large oak tree and a leg sticking out behind it. When I get closer, I can see Carter sitting at the base of it. One knee propped up with his arm over it, he's got the sunglasses on and seems to be looking up at the sky. With not much of a breeze, his hair stands up in its poof.

Getting closer, I notice he has earbuds plugged in. His foot taps along to the rhythm of whatever he's listening to. I don't know what I should do because I'm standing only a couple of feet away and he should see me, but he hasn't moved or said anything. I lean over and tap his shoulder.

"Oh," he says a little louder than necessary, before pulling out the earbuds. "Hey, Emma."

"Hey," I say, and he flashes a grin, revealing his dimple. "Sorry, I'm not disturbing you, am I?"

"No, not at all." He motions for me to take a seat.

Sitting down, it feels different than last time. We planned to meet then. This time I just sought him out. He stares at me a moment, expecting me to say something, probably wondering what I'm doing here. I'm starting to wonder the same thing. That's when I point to his phone.

"What are you listening to?"

He glances down at his phone and seems to get nervous. I'm not sure because the glasses are covering his eyes. "Oh, um, Empire of the Sun."

"Really?" My eyes jump to where his should be, but I only see my reflection in the lenses.

"Yeah."

Maybe it's because he seems nervous, but I start to feel more at ease. Enough so that I hold out my hand, asking for one of the earbuds. He smiles and gives it to me, and that's when I hear the song; *Walking on a Dream*.

"That's a good one."

"Yeah." He lifts his shoulders. "But I think my favorite is probably *I'll Be Around*."

"Really?"

I remember texting with Baller, and it was one of the nights we covered likes and dislikes. He said Empire of the Sun was his favorite band and we talked about which songs from them we liked. That was one of his.

"How come?"

"The lyrics." He looks away, and even though I can't see his eyes, it's like he's thinking of something specific. "They talk about running and chasing flames on a dare." He glances at me, giving me a half smile. "It feels like all I've been doing is chasing flames."

The way he says it sounds remorseful. Like he's made a mistake about things. Then I'm reminded of what Lana and Micah said about the rumors. Maybe he did make mistakes. Deciding to change the topic, I hand him back the earbud.

"What's yours?" he asks.

"*DNA*," I answer without pause and start reciting the lyrics.

As soon as I'm done saying them, I realize he's still holding my hand, and I nervously look away, taking my hand back. Trying to regain my focus, and the whole reason I sought him out, I look back at him. "You okay?"

"Yeah, I'm good."

"You sure?"

He peaks an eyebrow over the sunglasses. "Why, did you hear something?" I can't stop my cheeks from flushing. He reaches up and takes off his sunglasses. "I'm sure there's no hiding when it's plastered on my face."

"Holy crap." I see the black eye, and my hand instinctively reaches up, but I stop myself from touching his face. "So, it's true?"

"That all depends," he says, pulling out his other earbud, wrapping the cord around his phone. "If you've heard the story that I was hooking up with McCormick's girlfriend behind his back and my teammates jumped me after practice, then no. It's not true. But, if you heard we got into a fight after practice, then yeah. That one's true."

"That's the one. Only it was during practice."

He laughs. "No, it was after."

"Why?"

He lets out a long sigh, shaking his head. "Stupid rumors. Rumors that got out of hand. That I *let* get out of hand." He looks away, dejected.

"So, all the stuff about you and Sarah?" He shakes his head. "Wait, so Jeremy got mad at you because you *didn't* hook up with her."

He finally meets my eyes again. "Not so much that, but that I didn't tell him the truth. That I let him, and the other guys think it happened."

"Why'd you do it?" I throw my hand over my mouth. "Sorry, that's none of my business."

"It's okay." He smirks, staring at me. "Who are you, Emma?"

"What do you mean?"

"Like, who are you? What makes you up? What makes Emma, Emma?" he asks with a smile.

I stare down at the ground, unsure. "I've never really been asked that before." I look back at him, and he seems to enjoy that he's asked me something so peculiar. "I don't know. I guess I'm honest. Thoughtful. At least, I try to be. I like to look at the bright side. Jen says I'm a little too much of a Goody Two-Shoes, but it's okay because she evens out our friendship with her sluttiness. Her words, not mine."

Carter lets out a laugh and a full smile, one that draws me in.

"You are. I don't know about a Goody Two-Shoes, but honest. And thoughtful."

"Carter, you barely know me."

"Nah, I know you," he says with a smile. The look he gives me, it's as if he does. "But me? All that I know I am is basketball. I've played all four years. I'm good at it. Freshman and Sophomore year, I wasn't anything else. I didn't *have* anything else. Then in Junior year, before the season, I hooked up with a girl ..." He pauses, looking away and I see his Adam's apple bobble nervously. "Anyways, after that people thought I was cooler. It's so stupid. Even if I barely held hands with a girl after that, if the rumors started, I didn't do anything to stop them. Because with every new rumor, a new echelon of this cool persona I was building for myself grew. When the rumors started spreading about Sarah and me after homecoming, well ... I'm going to sound like a douche, but after homecoming, I was on another level."

"You're right." I look at him and smile. "That does sound douchey."

"Thanks." He laughs. "So, that's why I didn't say anything. That's why I let almost everyone believe the rumor. Rumors."

I don't know what to say or how to respond. I can't imagine people thinking of me a certain way and letting them believe it, just so I could get popular. But the way he explained it, it's just what it is. He let it happen. So people would think he's something he wasn't. Would I ever do that? I'd like to say no, but what if it was something I really wanted? What if letting people believe one thing about me helped me in my art? Or get into a great art school? I don't know.

"Can I ask you something?" Carter breaks the silence. "That day I met you here when you were waiting for someone. Did you ever meet them?"

Chapter 29

Carter

I don't know when I started holding my breath, but I finally realize I'm not receiving any oxygen as I wait for Emma to answer. When I walked past her and her friends in the quad, I had no idea how I was even going to approach her. I came to the oak tree, the one place I could find a little solace in the wake of everything being blown up in my face. I wanted to connect with her. I want her to know who I really am and not what all the rumors say I am. Then, to my surprise, she came and found me.

I have no idea why she's here, talking to me, but she is. And when she asked me about the rumors, I'd been more honest with her than I had been with anyone. Even Matt knew the truth, but I never told him why I let the rumors keep going and never put a stop to them.

I'm nervous when I admit to listening to Empire of the Sun, but I'm done trying to hide everything. I just have to figure out how much she still wants to meet Texting Me. And I'm scared to death that bringing up that topic will give her a reason to get mad at me. Again.

She shakes her head no and looks away.

"Sorry." I keep my eyes on her. "How come?"

She looks off into the distance. "I don't know."

"What do you mean?"

"I mean, he didn't tell me."

"He didn't tell you why he didn't meet you? What'd he say when you saw him later?"

"Well ..." She bites her lip, still not making eye contact with me. "I didn't see him later."

"Oh, does he not go here?"

"No, he does. He has calculus with Mr. Hilton."

"Oh, so you guys got calc together?"

"Well, no." She looks at me finally. She doesn't look upset, more like she's wondering why I'm asking. "I just know he has that class."

"Oh." I stare at her cautiously, knowing what I'm going to say next is going to be the biggest risk yet. "So, do I know him? What's his name?"

She blinks at me. Biting her lip again, I can tell she's debating with herself whether to tell me or not.

"You don't want to tell me?"

"No, it's just ..." she lets out an exasperated sigh, dropping her head. "I don't know his name."

"What?" I try to sound confused without sounding judgmental.

Picking her head up, she wrinkles her nose at me. "I don't actually know him."

"Come again?"

"Well, no, I know him. We've talked a lot, but ... only

through text. We've never met." She drops her head into her hands.

With her eyes covered I let myself smile at her cute awkward and nervousness. I quickly press my lips together, trying to hide the smile, as she looks back up. "Wow, okay. That's interesting."

"I don't know why I'm telling you this. And it's not interesting. It's stupid." She frowns.

"Why?"

"Well, at first it was *interesting*." She makes air quotes as she says it. "And I got to know him, or at least, I thought I did. But then he stood me up. That day I saw you, we were supposed to meet for the first time. I think that's why I was so mad and was a complete bitch to you. I'm sorry about that, by the way. I didn't mean it."

"Yeah, you did." I smile.

"Okay," she says after a pause. "I did, but now I know you a little better."

"Eh, you probably know me better than you think you do." *Easy, Carter.* She gives me a sideways look, unsure what I mean, and I remind myself to choose my words carefully. "So, he could be anyone?" I look behind her and see a guy walking down the corridor. "He could be that dude, right there?"

"No, he's not anyone." She gives me a determined look as I raise an eyebrow. "I don't know who he is, but I *do* know him. He's smart. And nice. And he's considerate."

A feeling of elation washes over me, knowing that's what she thinks of me. "Well, yeah. Except he didn't—"

"Don't bring it up again."

"Sorry."

I wait for her to continue but realize I may have crossed a line. She looks deep in thought, and I can't stand that she might be thinking about the day she thought I stood her up all over again. Feeling alone and betrayed.

I keep my eyes on her, speaking a little lower. "Hey, for what it's worth, it had to be an amazing catastrophe that he went through. I mean, if you two know each other as well as you say you do, if *I* knew you like that, I'd do just about anything to make sure I met you."

She stares at me, and I wonder if I've said too much. Even if she hasn't figured it out, I want her to know, and every fiber in my body is urging me just to tell her. Come hell or high water; I should just tell her it's me and let the chips fall where they may. But as soon as the thought of revealing myself enters my mind, the bell rings.

She looks away while I throw my sunglasses back on. Getting to my feet and extending my hand to her, she takes it and stands up. I don't want to let go. I want to hold her hand all the way back to class. For the rest of the day. For the rest of my life. But I loosen my grip, giving her the opportunity to pull her hand away. She does, but she smiles back up at me, and it warms me to the core.

"Feel free to walk ahead of me." I point to my left eye that's covered by my glasses. "If you don't want any more rumors started up."

She lets out a soft giggle. "I'm sure nothing can be as bad as the ones that are already out there."

"You don't know McCormick."

She grins, shaking her head. "Come on."

Chapter 30

Emma

The only word I can think of to describe the next few days is weird. Weird, because ever since Monday, I haven't received any more texts from Baller. Weird, because my Heartbreak painting has taken this bizarre turn, where I'm adding flakes of gold to it. Weird, because after history Carter has walked me to art class, even though his class is on the other side of campus. And weird, because he's also asked me more about Baller. What kind of things he likes. Why I think he's nice if I've never met him. Sometimes he jokes about his looks, and I reassure him that looks don't matter. Then he switches it to my looks.

"So, if you ever do meet him, you're not nervous, right?"

"I mean, a little. It would be like a blind date. You never know what they're gonna think, seeing you—" I feel my cheeks heat up. "I mean, meeting you for the first time."

"I can't believe it." He laughs. "You're nervous about if he'll like what he sees."

"Carter, it's not that unbelievable."

"Yes, it is, Emma." He's still laughing, holding on to his backpack.

I let out a defeated groan. "It's not like I'm one of the cheerleaders. Someone like Sarah, or Natalie, or any of them."

"Come on." He bumps his shoulder against mine.

"Sorry, I'm not trying to say I'm hideous. I know I look good." I feel my face go red again. "Wow, not that I'm conceited or anything, it's just, I know I'm not ugly."

"Knowing you're not ugly, isn't being conceited. It's being confident."

"That's what Jen says."

"She's right."

"Anyways, people like what they like, right? I could be a swimsuit model, and he may be into grunge girls who wear beanies and flannels."

He lets out another laugh. It's infectious and starts to make me smile. "Wow, been watching 90s movies lately?"

"Yeah," I shrug. "I watched Clueless on TV last night."

"That's a good one."

"But you know what I mean? People have types."

We get to the art building, and he leans against the wall, just waiting for the bell. As if he would remain there the entire day until I told him to leave.

"Well, he'd be an idiot to see you and not be interested."

There it is again. I know it's flirting. But the way Carter says it, it doesn't sound like it. It sounds like an honest statement. The kind your family tells you because they're so proud of you. Because they love you so much, they couldn't imagine anyone in the world not liking you. It's wholehearted, and as much as it makes me blush and spread warmth throughout my chest, I don't understand it. How can Carter act as if he knows me so well? Like he knows who I am, inside and out, and everyone in the world is crazy if they don't see it.

I push the butterflies away and say bye. He just stands there, grinning at me as he leans against the wall until I walk through the door.

Before class starts, Ms. Hales asks me to meet Micah at the gym again, in preparation for the art show and I don't know what I'm more nervous about - My artwork on display or showing up and seeing Carter in the gym again. Shirtless. Sweaty. Smirking at me.

Stop it, Emma.

It's not like I'm trying to think about him, but after the last couple days, my brain is frayed. He's not exactly flirting, but sometimes I think he is. He's asking me sincere questions. Not just regular stuff like how my day is, but asking about my art. Why I'm painting my abstract painting with the certain colors. He actually asked if I paint with emotions. Not colors, or brushes, or types of canvas. Emotions. It honestly threw me for a loop, making my stomach go queasy. In a good way.

"Interesting," Ms. Hales says, taking a step behind me as she looks at Heartbreak. "So, you've got all this torment and catacombs of clouds." She points to the bottom of the painting, where I've painted a cracking brick and a gold dahlia, the tips of the pedals are silver. "But then here, you have maybe the most important part."

"What do you mean?"

"This." She stares intently at the painting. "Chaos. Pain. It's swarming all around, but there's still something growing.

Still something beautiful, trying to reach out. It reminds me of love."

I stare at her, blinking.

"Love can be fickle. It can hurt, and torment, and sometimes we never want to feel it again. But deep inside, we do. Maybe not at first, if we've been hurt, but eventually there's something inside of us growing. Yearning. May I ask what you call it?"

It's not like she has to ask or be as polite as she is being. But that's Ms. Hales, and it's why she's my favorite teacher. It still doesn't help the shyness in my voice, as I look at the ground to answer her.

"Heartbreak."

She stands there as the seconds tick by. Finally, I feel like I have no choice and I have to look up to meet her eyes. She gives me a sincere smile and gently squeezes my arm. "Perfect."

After class, I meet with Jen outside of the gym, and I make a conscious effort to steady my breathing. I haven't told Jen that Carter has been walking me to class and I don't know how I'm going to try and stay calm when I see him. Now that all the rumors have unfolded and I'm getting to know him better, he seems like such a different person to me. Then again, I guess he was always that person. He just let the rumors change everyone's perception of him.

Jen gives me a flirty look, remembering the last time we were in the gym, and I smile back. It's no use, I'm feeling ... something. We walk inside and see Micah and Lana going over the paperwork, looking around.

"We got the whole gym to ourselves," he says triumphantly.

"Oh." I look around, and disappointment hits me.

"Yeah, they have an away game."

"Really? Carter was in history. He didn't say anything," I say, then immediately regret it, as Jen shoots me a look.

"Oh, you two must be getting close?"

"No." I bite my lip, avoiding eye contact. "He's just walked me to art a few times."

"A few times?" Her look goes from suspicious to slightly hurt. "Why didn't you tell me?"

"Jen, there's nothing to tell. He just does it for some reason. It's right after history. You know, the class we have together."

"Yeah, right. *For some reason.*"

"It's not a big deal."

"No, it's not. But you seem awfully disappointed he's not here today."

"I am not." I cross my arms.

Micah gives me a funny look, while Lana and Jen both look at me like I'm lying. I'm so not ready to have a conversation about liking Carter right now.

"Anyways, they're playing Beckman." Micah ignores our banter. "Since it's just across town, they didn't have to miss class." He looks around the gym. "Ms. Hales says we're gonna have ten to fifteen dividers. Each wall can hold anywhere from three to six paintings, depending on the size of the piece. You're the only person who's gone as big as six feet."

"Yeah, she likes 'em tall," Jen snarks, sticking her tongue out at me.

I groan, rolling my eyes. "You are so funny."

Chapter 31

Carter

I spend half the week trying to get to that moment I felt on Monday. The moment where I had Emma right in front of me, ready to tell her everything. That I'm BigBaller27. But I can't do it.

Walking her to class is something she doesn't seem to mind, so that's a good sign. I've been bringing Baller up, trying to see how much she still feels for him, er, me. I haven't texted her anymore because I'm focusing on trying to win her over as myself. On our way to her class, it finally hits me. The idea. A way to finally confess everything to her, if I can pull it off and that's a big if.

After history class, I wait for her as I have throughout the week. Only now she seems a little uneasy about it.

"Everything okay?" I ask.

"Yeah." She nods, then looks around. "You know, you

don't have to keep walking me to art. I know your last class is all the way across campus."

"I don't mind." I shrug. "I look at it as a win/win."

"Win/win?"

"I get a head start on practice after school, by running across campus before my last class *and* I get to hang out with a cute girl like you."

She blushes but rolls her eyes at me. I have to remind myself to play it cool. This plan is like walking a tightrope.

"Anyways, I was thinking about you yesterday." *Jeez, Carter. You're supposed to play it cool!*

"Really?"

"Yeah, um … I mean, about you and the art show."

"Oh." She seems confused. This is not off to a great start.

"Anyways, it's this Friday night, right?" She nods. "So, I was thinking, and I know this is none of my business but … I don't think you should wait for this Baller guy to ask to meet you."

"I don't know." She looks to the ground, shaking her head. "I was the one who brought up meeting him the first time. What if he bails again? What if he's decided he doesn't want to meet? It's not like he's been in contact all that much lately."

Shit. I was trying not to text her because I didn't want her liking him more than me. Which, on the one hand, makes complete sense and on the other hand makes absolutely no sense. I never thought about the possibility of her feeling like I didn't like her anymore because my texting had gone cold.

"Yeah, that is weird. But, it's your art show. I mean, you've been working on these pieces for a while, right?"

"Yeah."

"And it means something to you. So, maybe this would

light a fire under his ass or something, and he'll finally realize how special you are." She stops and stares at me as if trying to understand my words. "What?"

"It's just ... never mind."

"What?" I egg her on, smiling and bumping her shoulder.

"Sometimes, when you say things, you seem ... nothing. Forget it."

"What is it, Emma?"

She stops walking and turns to face me. "Okay, I'm going to do something totally out of character, and I need you to be honest with me?"

"Okay?" I reply nervously, wondering if she's figured everything out.

"Sometimes you say things, and I think you're," she swallows nervously, "ugh. Sometimes I think you're flirting with me. But then you stop, and you talk about this guy, who I don't know as if you're trying to hook us up?"

The words come out fast and when she stops speaking the redness in her cheeks is getting brighter. I take a breath. My words have to be honest. But I want her to like me, not Texting Me.

"Truth?"

"Truth."

"Emma, I think you're awesome. Amazing."

"And you'd know this how?"

"I just do." I let those words hang in the air, staring at her, wishing I could kiss her. She's so beautiful, inside and out. This plan has to work. It has to. "But, I know you don't see me like that. And you know my deal, all the rumors, and everything. If you like this Big Baller guy, then I say make a move. You should get everything you want, Emma."

She stares at me, her hot cheeks still uncooled. "Carter, you don't know what I see you as?"

I raise an eyebrow. "Really?"

Maybe she does like me. She bites her lip and looks like she's going to add something. Then the bell rings. A coy smile covers her lips, while I throw a tirade of expletives in my head at the bell.

"Saved by the bell, huh?" I curl a lip.

She lingers by the art room door a little longer, and I think the moment is still with us. Then her eyes widen as she looks around. "Shoot, you're late."

"It's okay."

"Go!" She pushes me away playfully. I can't resist grabbing her arms, holding on to her just a second longer than I need to before I head off to class.

I'm not sure when or even if she's going to text me, but with the art show only a day away, I'm hoping she does.

The two games we needed to win have turned into one. We lost to Beckman, and that should've knocked us out of contention to make the playoffs. But both University High and Corona del Mar High both lost in upset games. They should've wiped the floor with their opponents, but somehow didn't. That means our next divisional game is it. All or nothing.

We'll be playing the same day that Emma has her art show. As important as the game is, my plan with Emma is the most important thing because it's not a game. I'm doing my best to try and win her over and hoping everything plays out right. But a lot hinges on if she ends up asking him to come to the art show. And what her reaction will be to my answer.

Chapter 32

Emma

I stare at my phone for at least thirty minutes, trying to figure out what I want to do. If someone said at the beginning of senior year that I'd be debating on whether to invite a mystery guy to an art show or if I should pursue something with Carter Dixon—a something that seems to have appeared out of nowhere—I'd have called them crazy. I'd have laughed in their face, hysterically, and said they were deranged. But here I am, deliberating that exact scenario.

Did Carter really say he thought I was awesome? That I'm amazing? I don't know what exactly he's basing that off of. I've known him throughout high school, but we barely talked. How does he act like he knows me so well? And why do I honestly believe him? When he said I don't see him *that way*, I was glad he couldn't read my mind because I was staring at that dimple again, thinking how cute it looked.

How cute *he* looked. Is that why I've stared at his lips more lately?

After school, I'm still trying to decide what to do. It's not like I can text Carter and invite him to the art show, because I don't have his number, plus he has a game. I think it's an important one too if I remember from the school announcements. So that leaves Baller. Jeez, I still think that's a stupid name. And we haven't talked much. If I do ask him to meet again, what will he say? There's only one way to find out.

Emerald22: Hey
Emerald22: U still around? :)

I'm surprised by how fast he responds.

BigBaller27: Yep. Sorry, I've just been busy
Emerald22: Lots of school work?
BigBaller27: Something like that

I stare at my phone. What does that mean? If it's school work, wouldn't he just say that? Maybe he has a job? But why wouldn't he tell me that? Plus, he never mentioned having a job before. A sudden disapproval hits me.

BigBaller27: What's up?
Emerald22: So...

I grip my phone tightly, letting out a long breath.

Emerald22: U know how I'm in art?
BigBaller27: Yeah
Emerald22: Well, tomorrow night we have an art show. I have three paintings that are going to be shown

BigBaller27: That's awesome! :D
Emerald22: Yeah. Well...
Emerald22: If u still want to meet, I was wondering if you wanted to go?

Gritting my teeth, I stare at the screen. This is it; if he says yes and doesn't show up, then I'm over it. Why waste my time on someone who stands me up twice? But what if he says yes and *does* show up? Suddenly, I'm not sure what I want. Thinking about him saying yes and finally meeting him, I abruptly think of Carter. I like talking to him. And it seems like he likes me. No, he does like me. He told me so. I let out an unsure groan, not knowing what has happened to my life these last few weeks.

BigBaller27: Oh man, I'd love to! I really would, but I can't. I'm so sorry. I've been dying to meet u and was waiting for you to bring it up because I wasn't sure how badly I screwed up

I let out a sigh of relief. He can't make it. But wait, don't I want him to make it? Don't I want to meet him?

Emerald22: Ok, no biggie. Just thought I'd ask
BigBaller27: I'm serious. I want to meet u! If I could make it to the art show, I would :(

He does seem to be honest, and I'm not just reading into the frowny face emoji. My nerves a little more settled, I decide to put all the pressure on him.

Emerald22: Okay then. When u think of a time we should meet, u let me know

There. Now I'm not going to worry about it. If he wants to meet, then he'll have to bring it up. He'll have to pick a day and place. A strange calm takes over me. I'm not worried about meeting him, or if I ever do. He stood me up once, and now he's turned me down, even if he did say he wanted to go but can't.

BigBaller27: Will do ;)

He replies but I don't give it much more thought.

The next day at school, Micah is super nervous at lunch, while Lana tries to calm him down.

"It's just an art show," she says, running her fingers through his hair.

"You don't get it," he answers brashly, earning a scowl from her. "Sorry. Emma, explain please."

"It's like ..." I try to think of something Lana does and remember she writes for the school newspaper. "So, let's say you're working on some a new article, something you've worked really hard on. And now, you're going to throw it up for the world to see."

"I do that all the time with my blog."

I wrinkle my nose. "No, it's not the same. It's just different. We put our heart and soul into these pieces. Sometimes, without even thinking. Then we step back, and we're a little shocked we're putting as much of ourselves out there as we are. It's hard to explain."

"She's right," Micah says, seeming to have calmed down a bit. "The pieces I did, they tell my story. And yeah, everyone might not be able to see it. Some people will look at it and just see a tree or a bird. But what I'm doing? I'm putting my soul on that canvas, and it's nerve-wracking for people to see it, even if they don't get it."

She lifts her shoulders. "Okay, then."

It doesn't seem to faze her, but she doesn't seem aloof to Micah's concerns either. She leans against his shoulder, before wrapping her arms around him, kissing him.

I've been around them enough to witness much more PDA than I'm sometimes comfortable with, but something about this interaction, this closeness, strikes a chord in me. I want someone who gets me. I don't realize I'm staring until Jen pokes my arm.

"So, you invite anyone special to see your stuff? I mean, besides me of course."

"Yeah, but he can't make it."

"Holy shit. You asked Carter to come to the gallery?"

"What? No." I narrow my eyes at her, as Micah and Lana look on curiously.

"Then who are you talking about?"

Oh crap. I forgot I didn't tell her about the texts I sent. Feeling her mood shift, I glance to the side and see her reprimanding look. "Emma! You did not invite *him* to the art show."

"Who?" Lana asks.

"Mr. Big Baller, ugh! The loser-and-a-half who should no longer be invited anywhere!"

"I know." I groan. "But Carter said if I really wanted to meet him, then I should invite him. It'd show if he was serious or not."

"Carter said?" Jen's disapproving look turns into incomprehension, as she put her hands to her waist.

"Yeah." I look away.

"Speaking of Mr. Dixon," Lana says in a quieter voice. Her eyes move behind me.

I turn around and see Carter walking over to us, his gym bag hanging over his shoulder. He's still wearing the sunglasses even though most signs of the black eye have faded. I like them. He smiles, and I feel the butterflies. I can't deny that I'm feeling something for him.

"Hey, Carter," Jen calls out in an over-the-top, flirty way.

"Hey." If he notices her tone, he doesn't react to it. "Hey, Emma."

"Hi." I smile, breaking my eye contact with him, only to see Jen give me an impish grin.

"Um, can I talk to you for a second?" he asks.

"Right now?"

"Yeah." He looks around the quad. Is he nervous? Why would he be nervous? "I have to catch the bus to head out to the game against Northwood."

"Oh yeah," Micah says. "I hope you guys win. It'd be awesome if we finally make the playoffs before we graduate." Carter grimaces. "Sorry, I meant that in a good way."

"It's cool," Carter says, looking back at me.

"Um, yeah. Sure."

I motion for Jen to watch my stuff. I wish I didn't even look at her, because as I do, she licks her lips, before giving me a nod and wicked smirk. Micah stares at me cautiously, Lana raises her eyebrows, and my anxiety begins to build as we walk away.

"Sorry about—" I look back at Jen, who's now making fish lips at me. I give her a hostile stare, and she just winks at me. "That. What's up?"

"Hmm, oh, nothing. Sorry, um ..." He rubs the back of his neck.

"You know, you do that a lot."

"What?"

"Rub the back of your neck. Are you nervous?"

"Yeah, you could say that."

"Well, it's a big game."

"Right ... the game." He lets out a chuckle, but it doesn't sound right. If he isn't nervous about the game, what else would he be worried about? Surely, it isn't talking to me.

Wanting to keep the trepidation from building, I keep the topic on basketball. "You guys still have a game next week, right?"

"Yeah, but tonight's the big one. If we don't win, then we're done." I nod, and he seems to calm down. "But, anyway, I wanted to talk to you before I left. So, um, did you, uh ..." He bites the inside of his lip. Of course, that makes me stare at his lips now.

"You know?" he says, regaining my attention.

"Did I what?"

"Ask your texting-buddy? About going tonight? I wanted to see how it went."

I frown but not because of the answer Baller gave me. I'm not nervous or scared or apprehensive. I'm annoyed because I don't want to think about that guy.

Staring down at the sidewalk, we walk to the parking lot where the bus is waiting for him. I can't believe my thoughts. I'm not thinking about Baller at all. And I don't *want* to think about him. I want to be thinking about Carter. My shoulders tense and I try to remain calm as the revelation hits me.

"Oh, wow," I whisper, keeping my eyes on the ground.

"What?"

"Sorry." I let out a nervous laugh. "I, uh, I did ask him. He said he couldn't make it."

"That sucks." Carter's confidence seems to return. "He say why? Lots of homework, or something? Job?"

"No," I feel my confidence return also, annoyed with Baller all over again. "He just said he couldn't make it. I asked if he had a lot of school work, and he said, 'something like that'. What does that even mean?"

"That's lame," he says, giving me a worried look. "Sorry."

"No, it's okay. It is lame. Anyway, I told him whenever he wants to meet it's up to him now. I'm done chasing him."

"Good. You shouldn't chase anyone, Emma. Any guy worth anything should be the one chasing you."

There it is again. The assuredness. Only this time, as we stop near the fence of the parking lot, I stare at him. I want to really see him. The golden flakes that bounce off his light brown eyes. The same gold I added to my painting this week. I feel my cheeks get hot, but I can't look away. I didn't do it consciously, but looking at him now, I realize I'm adding bits of brightness to Heartbreak from my interactions with Carter. I can feel my breath quickening as I stare at him.

"Yeah, right." I try to play off his compliment.

He stares back, and I realize how close we're standing. My feet know what I want before my mind does, as I take a step closer to him. He welcomes the closeness, and I feel his hand under my chin, holding my gaze to his as if he's afraid I'll look away. The angst inside should force me to, but I don't want to. His hand reaches higher, as his thumb caresses my cheek.

"It's the truth, Emma." He whispers, leaning closer. "I'd chase after you."

I feel the warmth of his breath on my lips. And then his meet mine. It's soft. Timid. Like he isn't sure if I want him to kiss me. But I do. I really do. My hand grabs the sleeve of his jacket, pulling him closer. I feel the pressure of his lips, harder against mine.

Returning the fervor, his tongue slides across my bottom lip. My body tells my brain to step aside, and my arms instinctively reach up and wrap around his neck. My tongue meets his, and the electricity shoots through me. Then, like a bolt of lightning, a car horn shakes us both awake. Or rather, a bus horn.

Carter snaps his head to the side as someone yells out, "We don't have all day, Dixon!"

I blush and put my face into his chest, peaking over his shoulder to see what looks like his coach standing on the steps of the bus.

"You can kiss your girlfriend after we win tonight!"

Carter lets out a nervous laugh. "Sorry about that." I give him a confused look, unsure what he's sorry for. Reading my expression or my mind—maybe both—his hands grab mine. "About the interruption. Not the kiss. Are you?"

I shake my head, a smile curling on the edge of my lips. "No."

He takes a step towards the bus but still holds my hand. "I'll talk to you later. After the game."

"Okay," I nod again, the smile still on my face. It may be permanently attached.

Turning around, he walks to the bus. I can see some of his teammates scowling at him. Whatever happened, they must not all be over it. But from others, I can hear teases being shouted. As he takes a step on the bus, he turns around, giving me a small wave. I return the gesture and watch as the bus drives away.

It's only then that my brain finally catches up. A million questions race through my head, but two keep floating to the top. His coach said 'girlfriend'. Is that what I am now? Is Carter my boyfriend? The other question I wish I can forget. What am I going to do about Baller?

Chapter 33

Carter

There's no removing the smile from my face. Not during the bus ride to our game, in which Jeremy and others make stupid comments about me finally 'getting some'. Not as we pull into the parking lot of Northwood High and exit the bus, with all of Northwood's students giving us the evil eye. Not even during half-time, when we're getting chewed out by our coach, for being down by fourteen points.

Don't get me wrong; it sucks trying to do everything we can to beat Northwood, only to keep getting knocked back down. They're stronger and faster, one of the main reasons they have already secured a place in the playoffs. And as much as I want to win, I can't get the kiss out of my head. I can't keep the way Emma's lips tasted, or her intoxicating smell off my mind. It was everything I thought it would be and more and there's no way in hell I'm letting her go now.

Now all I have to do is finish the plan, finally confess I'm Baller and hope she still wants me.

"This is it!" Coach yells at us as we huddle around, only ten seconds left in the game. "We're down by four. Two possession game. It's now or never. McCormick, you post up, and we run the three." Coach circles some x's on his dry-erase board. "Mitchell, you take the shot or dump it off to Dixon. Just like we practiced, boys!" I look over at Lucas, who I know will take the shot if he needs to.

The referee whistles for us to get going and Matt throws the ball to Lucas. He dribbles around a defender and stops, about to take the shot, but a new defender jumps to block him. He throws me the ball, and I shoot it, sinking a three-pointer.

Northwood gets the ball and Matt runs over to foul them, stopping the clock. It's our last foul to give in the game, so Northwood isn't going to get a foul shot. But we need a steal and to score again, or else that's it.

They throw the ball in and try to delay the clock. With only six seconds left, we have to steal it without a foul. Matt runs to defend, but the player throws the ball to his team-mate right in front of me. I dart towards the ball, my fingers making just enough contact to deflect it. Everyone scrambles as the clock ticks down to three.

Matt and Lucas run ahead, as I dribble towards the hoop. All we need is two points. A simple lay-up can get us the win. Northwood's defenders catch up and get in front of me, blocking me from the basket. Lucas is open at the top of the key, so I throw him the ball. It barely touches his fingers before he jumps in the air and lets it go. The game clock winds down and a buzzer sounds through their gym.

Time seems to slow. Everyone in the gym—our team,

their team, everyone in the stands—we all hold our breath. As the buzzer goes off, the ball floats in the air towards the hoop and hits the back of the rim. More collective gasps, as the ball bounces up, before falling back down towards the front of the hoop. It hits the front of the rim. Then it bounces away.

Northwood doesn't need a win to celebrate, but that doesn't stop what seems like their entire student body from running on to the floor, everyone screaming in elation. Through the commotion on the court, we carry out our obligatory handshake with the other team, before heading to the locker room.

"What the hell, Carter?" Jeremy yells.

"Shut up, Jeremy!" Matt shouts back.

"He had the shot!"

"No, he didn't! Thirty-five was all over him."

"Bullshit!" Jeremy gets in my face, but I'm done fighting with him. "You were right there for the layup. You too much of a pussy, you can't score with girls that you can't even score baskets anymore?"

Okay, maybe I'm not done fighting with him. I jump up, grabbing his jersey, and slam him into the lockers. Before anything significant can happen, the rest of the team starts shouting, getting between us.

"Enough! Enough!" Coach steps in. He turns to Jeremy, wrapping a fist around his jersey, then does the same to me. "Listen up!" His head dances around, leering at the rest of the team. "All of you! You played your best, all of you did. This is a tough loss, but you gave it all you had. McCormick hit the showers. Mitchell, Hillard? You two keep an eye on Dixon." Coach's eyes flash between Jeremy and me again. "I don't know what the hell's gotten into you two, but you need to man up. We still have one game left, and I'll be damned if we lose our last game of the season in front of our home crowd."

I keep my distance the rest of the time and after the showers. Matt and I sit in the back of the bus as we make our way back to school. Plugging my earbuds in, I turn on my music and try to forget the game, remembering what I'm going back to. I'm counting on getting back in time for the art show, and thankfully we make it back to the school thirty minutes before it ends.

"Where are you going?" Matt asks as I walk towards the gym instead of my car.

"I'm gonna check out the art show." I motion to the gym.

"Hope it works out."

"Thanks, me too."

Walking into the gym, large dividers are set up all over the basketball court. The show has been open for nearly two hours, but there are still students and parents mingling, looking at different paintings. Some of the dividers are set up adjacent to one another, while others form corners. It almost resembles a tiny maze you can walk around. I don't see Emma as I come in, so I decide to walk through, looking for her while checking out the artwork.

Turning a corner, I see a painting of palm trees on a beach and find Micah's name signed at the bottom. On a neighboring divider sits another piece by him and a few other paintings.

I keep walking and see a gorgeous waterfall painting. It has vibrant blues and greens and looks like something out of a rainforest. In the corner are initials and I know they're Emma's because next to the waterfall piece is an abstract painting exactly how she described it. It's our school colors, different shades of red and gold, with triangles and circles. I know she has a third painting, but there are two more next to hers with different initials. That's when I turn around and see a six-foot painting behind me. The bottom corner has her initials on it. I stand there, gazing at the piece.

All her thoughts about paintings and how they can invoke feelings suddenly hit me. I never thought something like that would, but it does. It's a scene of sorts. Different shades of blues, grays, and dark greens. Above, sits a huge dark purple cloud with what looks like burgundy lightening in it. There's a long, dark red lightning bolt, shooting out from the cloud, towards a small flower that's growing out of a brick. I've never examined art. I never tried to interpret it or figure out what the artist is trying to say, but for some reason, this painting speaks to me. It's hurting.

The cloud is pain, and the pain is shooting out towards this delicate flower down below. And even though the background is swirling around, chaos rushing around the canvas, the small flower stands fearlessly. Preparing for whatever the storm is bringing. Then I see what I missed before with all the other paintings. A little tag on the wall, citing the artist's name and the name of the piece.

"Heartbreak," I whisper to myself, immediately feeling horrible.

Heartbreak? Did she decide to paint this when she thought I stood her up? Is this how she felt that day? How long after did she keep feeling like this?

"Carter?"

Emma stands behind me. Her usually straight black hair has slight curls in it, and she's wearing a dark green skirt that sways around her legs, cutting off at the knees. She looks adorable and sexy at the same time. My eyes drink her in, but I can't overcome the sinking pit in my stomach.

"What are you doing here?"

"Oh." I look around. "The bus dropped us off, and I know it's your art show tonight. I thought I'd check it out."

"Really?" She beams. Her fingers fiddle with one another and a cute rosiness hits her cheeks.

"Yeah," I say, trying to bat down my guilt.

I remember our kiss earlier and offer my hand to her. She looks at it nervously. For a split-second, I think I dreamed what happened before. That I was off in la-la-land, only wishing that we shared that kiss. But she calms my fears, taking my hand.

"This is amazing." I look back at the painting.

"Really? You like it?"

I nod, then motion to the tag. "Heartbreak? How come you named it that?"

I try to keep my hand from squeezing hers too tightly, as the fear builds back up. When she doesn't answer at first, I look over to see the hesitation on her face. I know what she's going to say before she says it.

"I decided to paint it a little bit ago. That day you saw me in the courtyard."

"It's so ... powerful."

"I have a confession." She looks over at me, giving me a slight smile.

"Oh yeah?"

"This piece is about you." My eyes widen. She finally figured it out. "I mean, not totally. But a piece of it, um, you kind of inspired." She seems calm. And she's still holding my hand. Would she be doing that if she knew? "You see the flower?"

"Yeah."

"That's you." My fears halt, replaced by curiosity. "Sorry, you're not the flower." She giggles. "I mean, this whole thing, it is powerful. But, um ..." She looks down at our intertwined fingers, gripping my hand a little tighter. "Well, okay, the flower is me. And the gold and silver in it? That's you."

I look back at the painting and see all the chaos and confusion of it. Then the flower, lined with gold and silver. It reminds me of strength. Hope. Does she mean I give her hope? Me, Carter? Not Baller? I grin as my confidence returns.

"So, the flower's you?" I ask, and she nods. "And I'm the silver and gold *in* the flower?" I arch an eyebrow, making her cheeks blush.

"Oh my God, Carter!" She slaps my arm. "That's so not what I meant."

"Sorry." I laugh. "So, I'm *on* the flower."

She pulls her hand away, crossing her arms. She shoots me an angry stare, but her smile tells me she isn't really mad. "Again, not funny."

"I'm kidding." Pulling her closer, I'm pleasantly surprised by how natural it feels. And how easy her arms wrap around me. "Seriously. It's beautiful. You're beautiful."

Leaning over to kiss her, I'm not sure who is around, but I don't care. Her hands come to my face, and the skin warms where her fingers touch my cheeks. The smell from when we kissed earlier returns, and I never want to forget it. Our lips only touch for a moment before someone clears their throat behind us.

"Didn't you two get enough of that during lunch?"

Emma breaks away, embarrassed. I grin at her shyness, before looking over at Jen. "Wait, how do you—"

"BFF," Jen says proudly. "And not that I like interrupting my bestie playing tonsil hockey, but Ms. Hales is asking for you, Emma."

I smirk as I watch Emma's reaction. She looks like she

wants to rip Jen's hair out. They're complete opposites, but I can see why they're best friends. They even each other out.

"I guess I better go." Emma looks up at me with a disappointed look.

"Yeah, I better get home." I hold on to her hand, as Jen walks away. "I'll see you on Monday."

"Okay." She smiles, and I lean over and give her one more kiss. Taking in another breath of her scent, I hope it'll tide me over for the weekend.

Getting to my car, I gaze down at my phone. The endgame is in sight. I'm glad she didn't remember to ask for my number. Hopefully, she won't ask anyone else for it. I've won her over, and now it's time for the final stage of my plan —revealing myself as Baller. I'm just praying that once that happens, she doesn't go back to hating me.

Chapter 34

Emma

To say I'm on cloud nine would be an understatement. Maybe cloud ninety? Nine hundred? As soon as I reached the lunch table the day of the art show, I spilled my guts to everyone, not just Jen. I couldn't help it. I was bubbling over. Micah looked at me like a concerned older brother, while both Lana and Jen fawned and squealed with excitement. I kissed Carter! Carter kissed me! And if that wasn't enough, then he went out of his way to visit the art show. And we kissed again! It's insane, and I'm most shocked by the fact that I didn't act like a blubbering idiot. Probably because other than these past few weeks, I've only ever treated him like a sleaze-ball flirt, something I do feel a little bad about now because we're ... I don't know. A thing!

Jen spends the night at my house after the art show, and then we hang out with Lana over the weekend, since her parents are out of town.

"I still can't believe I missed it." Lana groans while we lay out next to her pool. "Twice."

"It's not like we scheduled it to happen," I say. "Hey, was Micah mad you weren't at the show?"

Micah and I were both excited about the art show, and Lana was planning on going, but I guess she texted him last minute and told him she couldn't make it. He seemed upset the entire night. He even left the show early, only staying for half of it.

"Yes." She lets out a frustrated sigh that seems more angry than apologetic.

"You guys good?" Jen asks.

"I don't know. He's just so ... serious. Always painting or working on his graphic novel." Lana keeps her eyes closed as Jen and I stare at each other. "I mean, I knew he was really into his art before we started dating, but he just seemed like the quiet and mysterious type, you know?"

"Not to mention, he is hot," Jen says playfully.

"Jen," I groan. Being friends with him since the beginning of high school, we've always had a brother/sister relationship.

"Oh, come on, Emma." Jen swats my arm as she sits up and grabs her drink. "I know you always say he's like a brother, and yeah, I do too. But now that you've got Carter Dixon's tongue to play with, you can't tell me Micah's not hot."

I scrunch my lips together. "Okay, he is attractive. In a totally platonic, sibling, kind of way."

"Wow, Emma." Jen wiggles her eyebrows. "I never knew you were into incest. You kinky girl, you."

My brow furrows and my jaw drops because even for Jen, that's too much. Before I can say anything, Lana gets up from her seat and dives into the pool. Swimming over to the ledge, she reaches over for her sunglasses, crossing her arms over the ledge.

"Anyways, it's getting to be a little much now. We're eighteen—"

"Almost." I raise a finger.

"We're all almost eighteen. We only have a few months of high school left before we start college, but it's like he's already in college mode, and it's always work, work, work."

She lets out a sigh as Jen and I exchange another look. I don't think either of us has ever heard Lana say something negative about Micah, and we both know Micah adores her. Thankfully, she either doesn't feel the awkwardness or ignores it, and changes the subject.

"Enough about Micah. I want the gossip." Lana looks over at me, as I lay back down on the pool chair. "So, you guys are, like, a couple now?"

"I don't know." I try not to sound confused, even though I am.

Yes, he kissed me. He's been honest and sweet with me, and he even made an effort to go to the art show, which I didn't know at the time, but I'm sure it couldn't have been easy. People were talking about their basketball loss on Facebook and Twitter the next day, and I found out that since they lost the game, they weren't making the playoffs. That has to suck. He could've just went home and tried to forget about it, but he didn't. He came and saw me. He told me I'm beautiful. It's all things a boyfriend would do, isn't it? But we didn't talk about what we are. We just ... are.

"You got his number, right?" Lana asks, breaking me from my train of thought.

"No," I grumble, more in disappointment at myself for not thinking of it.

"I'm telling you," Jen laments, "let me just text one of his friends. I've been dying for a reason to get Franco's number."

"No!" I scold her. "I told you, I'll just get it Monday. I don't want to come off as clingy or needy."

"You guys kissed. Twice. You should have his number."

"And I will, on Monday. Which is tomorrow by the way. It's not that big of a deal."

Jen's eyes widen with anticipation. "Does this mean he's going to be sitting with us during lunch? Can you ask him to bring over some of his friends?"

I'm about to chide her again when my phone goes off. Reaching for it, I gasp as I see the notification. The only other thing that's been on my mind, other than the amazing kisses I've shared with Carter, is Baller. And not in a good way. He seems like a nice guy even if he did stand me up. But since then, he's been distant. And now with Carter, I have no idea what to tell him. But I know I have to end it. I can't keep up a secret conversation with someone I don't know if I'm going out with Carter.

BigBaller27: How's ur weekend?
Emerald22: Good

One word answers. That's what I'll do. Just keep it short, sweet, and to the point. Hopefully, he'll get the message and just fade away. Yes, not mature at all, but I don't want to have to tell him not to text me anymore. It just seems mean.

BigBaller27: Just good? No big plans? No fun parties?
Emerald22: Nope

"Who is that?" Jen scowls at me. From her look, I know she knows.

"No one."

"Right."

"What? Who is it?" Lana asks.

"It's no one." I hold my phone tighter, hoping she gets the message.

"It's the stand-up jerkoff."

"You're still texting him?" Lana asks, but it's not as accusatory as Jen. "Would you consider that cheating?"

"What?" My eyes shoot to her. "No. Absolutely not. For one, I'm not doing anything. I don't even know him. And two, I'm trying to figure out how to end our conversations."

"Just tell him to drop dead," Jen says.

"Jen, I—"

My phone chimes again.

BigBaller27: Ok

BigBaller27: Hey, so do u like basketball?

I gape at the screen, trying to keep my head from exploding. No, this isn't cheating. It's not. But why do I feel like I'm cheating on Carter when Baller brings up basketball? Because Carter loves basketball and now, talking about it with someone I once liked, feels ... weird.

Emerald22: Why would u ask me that?

New worries sprout in my mind. Did he actually show up that day and see Carter? Does he know who I am and that Carter and I are a thing? Oh no, maybe he's one of Carter's friends.

BigBaller27: Just curious. I wanted to meet u finally. I

thought we might meet at our basketball team's last game tomorrow?

No. No, this is not happening. I can't let this happen.

Emerald22: I don't think that's a good idea
BigBaller27: :(
BigBaller27: Y not?

I just need to tell him. Just put it out there. He'll understand, right?

Emerald22: Look, I liked u. But...
Emerald22: Recently I've been talking to someone else. I don't think it's a good idea if we meet anymore
BigBaller27: Damn. I guess I blew it, huh?

See? Even in that text, he doesn't come off as spiteful. He seems cordial. Understanding. It almost freaks me out how well he's taking it.

BigBaller27: Is he nice?
Emerald22: No

I smile, knowing exactly what I'm typing, but he replies before I can send my next text.

BigBaller27: What???
Emerald22: He's amazing. He's great.

A smile cements on my face, remembering Carter's kisses.

BigBaller27: I'd still really love to meet u? Plz
Emerald22: No, I'm sorry. I don't see the point
BigBaller27: Just to know who u r. Plz plz plz. U can even bring ur friend who threatened to kick me in the nuts. I'd just really like to meet u finally. Maybe we can just be friends

"Seriously, you need to stop texting that dill-hole." Jen curls her lip, which makes me smile after seeing the last text he sent.

"He wants to meet."

"You cannot be serious."

"Do it." Lana gives me a mischievous smile.

"No!" Jen yells at her, and I'm a little taken aback. If anything, I'd have thought Jen would be the one egging me on to meet him. "Emma, you will not meet that asshole. You're going out with Carter now."

"Am I though?"

"What?" She scoffs. "Okay, you're not *boyfriend/girlfriend*." She uses air quotes. "You may not be, like, official but I saw you guys Friday night. You're together."

I nod. "Yeah, you're right. What's wrong with me? This is so stupid."

"But don't you want to know who he is at least?" Lana asks.

Jen gives her a warning look, as I stare back at my phone. It's not like I don't want to know. I've wanted to know for nearly a month. But the more time has gone by, the less important it's become. My eyes jump back and forth between Jen and Lana, who seem to be the little angel and devil that sit on your shoulders. Scrolling back through our text conversation, I see my reply about Carter. How he's nice and great. I'd hate for him to find out I'm meeting someone, who I honestly don't really want to meet anymore. Then I get an idea.

Emerald22: Fine. I'll meet u if the guy I'm talking to is okay with it.
BigBaller27: I'll take it :)

He immediately replies, and I smile at my phone, thinking how this will be over and done with tomorrow. What guy wants his girl meeting some random guy? Then I melt a little inside, imagining Carter thinking of me as his girl.

Chapter 35

Carter

"You what?"

Emma looks at me like I drowned a bag full of kittens.

"Yeah, I think you should do it," I answer her again, doing everything humanly possible to stay calm when all I want to do is break out in hysterics.

I keep a firm grasp on her hand as we walk because even though this is all part of my plan, I don't want her to feel like I'm saying she should just randomly go off and meet some mysterious guy. I want to come off as confident like I have nothing to worry about. But the way she's looking at me, I know I need to be very careful.

After I finished eating lunch, I walked over to the quad and met up with her. Jen nearly choked on her food as I approached their lunch table. The rumors about me have died a bit, but there's still a ton out there. The biggest one now is about the numbers of girls I asked to lie about hooking up with me. Whether she believes any of them or not, Jen still looks at me like I'm the biggest player in school, which earns me a smirk when I ask if I can sit with them.

My plan is to ask her to go to my last game, this time as me and not Baller. We head to history, and before I have a chance to ask her, she brings up the text message conversation. She seems at ease about it and is practically force feeding me reasons why she shouldn't go. Her eyes nearly fall out of their sockets, when I tell her she should meet him. My exact words are, "Yeah, that'd be cool. You should meet him."

I didn't think my plan all the way through.

"You think I should do it?" She stops walking, looking slightly confused. "You think I should meet him?"

"Yeah. What's the big deal? It's just some random guy, right?"

"I guess."

"I mean, you're not into him, are you?"

"Well, no, but ..."

"But what?"

After looking down for a moment, she raises her head and meets my eyes. The hurt I saw the day she thought I stood her up is there. Damn it. If she thinks that I don't care that she goes off and meets him, she might think I don't like her that much, or at all. That I'm not even the tiniest bit jealous if she meets some guy, which is entirely false. Because if this were a real conversation, about meeting someone I didn't know, I'd probably flip my shit and want to chain myself to her. The jealousy writhes through me just thinking about it.

"Sorry." I let go of her hand, wrapping both arms around her, pulling her closer. "I didn't mean to sound like it isn't a big deal. I guess I just trust you."

"What are we?"

Her blunt question makes me raise my eyebrows. "What are we?"

"Look, I'm trying not to be *that* girl, but I thought you liked me. I mean, I like you, and—"

"You like me?" I cut her off with a smile.

"Yes." She starts to blush, shaking her head. "I mean, you do like me, right?"

She looks away, but her directness is something I've grown fond of. I always appreciated how she seemed to say what she meant when we texted. I guess it's easier to sound much more confident through digital words than it is through vocal ones.

I put a finger under her chin, bringing her eyes back to meet mine. I wanted to save these words for her when I finally surprised her at the game, but I can't hold it back. I have to tell her.

"No," I whisper. "I think I'm in love with you."

I don't know what kind of reaction I was expecting from her, but standing there frozen, is not something I thought would happen. She blinks, so I know she's not catatonic, but now I feel like I've made a colossal mistake. Maybe it's too soon. No, it's not too soon for me. I know this girl. I'm in love with this girl. *Shit, what do I do?*

"You what?" she says, but it's so low I can hardly hear it.

"Sorry." I keep my eyes locked on hers, afraid if I look away she's going to disappear. "Was that too soon?"

"Too soon? Too Soon?" Her voice gets louder, and with each second, she's coming back to life. She looks utterly baffled. "Carter, how can ... you barely know me."

"No." I shake my head. "I know you. And you know me."

"What are you talking about?" More of her confidence is returning, and I'm not sure if she's getting mad or annoyed. "I've known who you are, sure. But I don't *know* you."

"Emma, you know better than almost anyone."

"That doesn't even make sense." She pulls her hands up to my chest. It's still a good sign that she hasn't backed away from me, right? "Okay, you ... you ..." I smile as her cheeks get red. "You feel that way about me, which is a whole other topic I think we need to talk about later, but this is so confusing."

"What?"

"If you feel like that, why are you so okay with me meeting this mystery guy. It doesn't make any sense!"

No shit. I really need to think these things out better. My brain scrambles, trying to think of something. "Well, um, it's my game."

"What?"

"It's my last game. I'll be there. I want to see who this guy is myself." Yeah, this could be viable. "I want you to meet him and that way, I can see who he is, and then he can see how badly he screwed up. I might not sound jealous, but that's only because I believe in us. I'm telling you, Emma, I really—"

"Don't say it."

I smirk. "Like you."

"Okay, fine. What if this guy shows up and I take one look at him, and I'm awestruck. I'm hit with love at first sight. What then?"

It's almost painful how hard I'm trying not to smile because I'd love it if that happened. If, when I finally reveal myself, she throws herself into my arms and tells me she loves me back. But no, I can't laugh or smile or even grin at her worry. I need to act like I'd be jealous. I try to think of her feeling like that for someone else, and it's easier to get into that mindset.

"Screw that," I spit out.

"See?"

I don't know how long we've been standing by the building until the bells sounds, letting us know lunch is over, and it's time for our next class.

"Okay, am I jealous? Yes. But maybe I just don't want you doubting yourself. Like, second-guessing, or something."

"What do you mean?"

"You know, that 'what if' mentality?" I pull her closer, and she seems a little hesitant. "I just don't want you to say, 'what if' later." She stares at me with a befuddled expression. "Come on, we're gonna be late for class."

Chapter 36

Emma

What the hell just happened? I walk into history, and I can't stop looking across the room at Carter. First, he acted like it isn't a big deal for me to meet some guy I've been texting. He actually said it was a good idea and that I should do it. Then, he told me he loved me? What? I'm not one to shy away from love, but still! He barely knows me but insists that he does. And that I know him.

Throughout the entire conversation, my insides were twisting like a pretzel because now I'm second guessing what I'm feeling. I mean, I like him, that much I know. But is it more than that? The conversations we've had between classes and at lunch have been nice. And I can't ignore how it feels when we kiss. It's like his lips were made to fit mine.

Then I remember how I felt about Baller. We talked so much. We had no physical contact, and we didn't even see each other, but by the time I was going to meet him I was falling. Hard. That's why I was so devastated when he didn't show. If only I could combine my long conversations I had with Baller and the epic gorgeousness of Carter.

Stop being ridiculous, Emma.

Plus, I shouldn't be thinking like that, should I? That really would be like cheating, right? I look back over at Carter, as he takes notes on something Mrs. Yanick is talking about. He looks over and gives me that incredible smile. It's like he only sees me. It makes my insides go all gooey. But if that's how he feels, and if he really does love me, then why is he so calm about me meeting Baller. Ugh, it's an infinite conundrum, and all I can do is keep going around and around.

Once the bell rings, I make my way outside where Carter's waiting in his usual spot to walk me to class. As I start to walk, he grabs my hand.

"Hey, I have to get to class early. I need to go over some stuff with Matt."

"Oh." I look over his shoulder and Matt gives me a friendly wave. "Okay."

"Look, I'm sorry about everything I said at lunch. Meet him or don't, it's up to you. I know I don't seem jealous, but I just really—" I raise my eyebrow at him, unsure what he's going to say, and he smirks. "Like you. And I thought you said you liked me too?"

"I do like you."

"Good," he says, smiling. "Then, I want you at the game."

"What?"

"Not to meet some douchebag that didn't meet you. I mean, seriously, how in God's name could anyone who's talked to you for two minutes, whether it's just text or not, not want to meet you?" Okay, see, that sounds like something I thought he'd say originally. "But I want you there. For me."

"Really?" I smile up at him as he wraps his arms around me.

"Yeah. You asked me a question earlier, and we kind of got off topic."

"I did?"

My brain is crammed with Carter's declaration of love, his nonchalant attitude over a mysterious guy wanting to meet me, and now how he's acting so adorable and sweet. I thought girls were supposed to be the confusing ones.

"You did. You asked what we were?"

"Oh yeah."

"Well, we're together. If that's okay with you?" He waits for my answer, nervousness across his face as if he thinks I'll actually say no. I nod and smile. "So, then, I'd like my *girlfriend* at my last game of the season."

Okay, I'm not saying I'm in love. I'm not. At least, I don't think I am. But the way he's staring at me, the smile he gives me, the way he's holding me close to him. All topped off by him calling me his girlfriend? Some serious heartstrings are being pulled.

"I'll be there then," I say, my grin stretching from ear to ear. "To see my *boyfriend*."

My words light him up, brighter than a Christmas tree. He leans in closer, bringing a hand to my cheek. Our eyes lock for a moment before I stare at his lips. Leaning closer to kiss me, I'm not concerned about who's looking, who's whispering, or what rumors are going to be spread. I'm not worried about anything because everything about his lips against mine feels perfect.

When he breaks away, I try not to frown, wanting to kiss him forever.

"I'll see you tonight at the game." He smiles and gives me another kiss, much too fast for my liking, before he walks away with Matt.

I'm beaming as I walk to art, feeling all warm and fuzzy inside. When my phone vibrates, I pull it out, and my mood suddenly shifts.

BigBaller27: So? What do u say?

I let out a groan because I'm really over this guy now. Especially since Carter just called me his girlfriend. The thought brings back my smile.

Emerald22: No. I'm sorry, but I can't do that
BigBaller27: Okay :(
BigBaller27: Jeez, this must be a good guy. Are u two in love or something?

I don't know what it is about the text, but I don't like it. It sounds condescending, even though he's never come across like that before. Knowing how Carter feels, something else hits me. I don't know that I'm in love with him right now, but I could be in the future. I know I shared personal things with Baller in the past, but that was the past. Then he stood me up. It's none of his business who I'm in love with, or not. *Like.* Who I'm in like with.

Emerald22: That's none of ur biz
BigBaller27: I know. I'm sorry :(
BigBaller27: Okay, I tell you what. If u do show up, I'll be there
Emerald22: I will be there because the guy I'm seeing is my bf now. He's on the team

Why do I feel compelled to tell him that? Maybe because then he'll get the hint that these text messages should end. I'm about to delete the messages, as the next text comes in.

BigBaller27: He's on the team?! Wow…
BigBaller27: Well, there are some cool guys on the team. I know Lucas Mitchell
BigBaller27: Just please don't tell me it's Carter Dixon or Jeremy McCormick. Those two are doucheheads

My mouth drops as I stop outside the art room, letting out a loud scoff.

Emerald22: Y r u being such an ass?
Emerald22: I already told you I'll be there and I have a bf. As far as I'm concerned, we're done talking!
BigBaller27: Ur right. I'm sorry. Plz don't be mad :(

I don't answer.

BigBaller27: Plz :'(

I want to be upset because he's never been so rude before, but my default mode kicks in, looking at it from his side. What if he was telling me he had a girlfriend now, and I was the one pushing to meet still? Would I be feeling the same thing as him? Probably.

Emerald22: It's fine. But srsly, I don't think we should text anymore. I'm sorry
BigBaller27: :(
BigBaller27: I understand. If you want to meet at the game

though, just to find out and be friends, I'll be there. I'll be wearing a wearing a red headband

I walk into the art room and stare at my phone as the bell rings. I feel like I should type back. Maybe tell him not to go or that I won't be looking for him. But I don't text anything back. Instead, I finally delete our entire conversation and his number.

"But what if I see him?" I ask, fidgeting with my hoodie, as Jen sits on my bed.

I told her everything. How Carter and I are official now, and he wants me at the game, but how Baller also texted me and said he'd be there too. The only thing I didn't tell her is that Carter told me he loved me, because ... I don't know. It rattled around my brain the rest of the day, and now that we're about to go to the game, I still don't know how to feel about it. I'm not freaked out. I know we seem to have a connection, but am I in love? The question returns my thoughts to Baller who, even though I deleted all of our text messages, I still feel a connection with too. Which is why I'm freaking out over him being at the game.

"Then ignore him," Jen commands, as she gets up from the bed and browses through my makeup. "You'll know who *he* is, and he won't know who you are. But honestly, I want you to point him out to me, okay?"

"Why?"

"I wasn't kidding, Emma." She gives me a serious look. "That guy is gonna get kicked so hard he might never be able to have kids."

Laughter bubbles out. I'm well past being angry at him

for standing me up, so even if I do see him, I don't think I'll tell Jen who he is. I don't hate him that much.

When we get to the gym, I scan everyone for a red headband. Even standing in line to get our tickets, I keep looking around, cursing myself every time I do, because I don't know what I'll do if I see him. Just ignore him? Go over and introduce myself? I have no idea.

Once we get inside, I'm still scanning the crowd, so it doesn't register that our team and the other school is on the court. Not until Carter comes running over.

"Hey, gorgeous," he says quickly, running by me with a basketball.

I spin on my heels, keeping my eyes locked on him. He stops running and jumps, shooting the ball. I want to say he makes it, but I have no idea because my eyes are solely on him. His shoulders glisten as he keeps his arms raised. He turns back around, looks over at me and grins, giving me a wink. My knees wobble.

"Okay," Jen tugs at my arm and gets me moving again. "Someone's gone lovesick."

If I were thinking more coherently, I would shush her, but I'm not. As we find seats in the bleachers, I can't stop watching him run around the court. Once the game starts, it's the same.

I don't know the rules of basketball. I know the teams go back and forth, shooting the ball, trying to score points. That's pretty much it. But even knowing next to nothing about the game, I'm transfixed. I keep my eyes glued to the court, watching Carter as he runs around, passing and shooting the ball. I know who some of the other players are, like Matt and Lucas. But for the most part, my eyes are locked on Carter.

"Emma, if you keep staring like that, you're gonna burst into flames." Jen pokes me in the ribs.

"Sorry." I finally break my line of sight, feeling my cheeks get hot.

"It's all good, girl. Franco looks amazing out there."

I find Franco on the court, and I can admit he is good looking. He has black hair that's trimmed in a buzz cut, and he's definitely fit, but it's not the same as Carter. The hair that's usually poofy on top has become sweaty, sticking to his forehead.

"Hey, so have you seen him?" Jen asks.

"Who?" I reply, still watching the court.

She laughs. "Girl, you're helpless. Douchey Doucherson."

Her words bring me back to reality. I totally forgot about Baller. Anxiety builds again, and I scan the crowd, looking for someone with a red headband. I'm not sure why he would be across the court, on the visitor's side, but I look over at the small crowd. Still nothing.

"I don't see anyone."

"Yeah, me either. What a sleaze. He didn't even have the balls to show up again."

"Whatever."

"You're okay with it?"

"You know what? I am. I was so wrecked that day he didn't show up. But now," I look at her and smile, "I'm not. It's no big deal."

She lets out a loud laugh. "That's because you're falling head over heels for Carter."

I don't disagree. I don't even get embarrassed. I just give a small nod and lift my shoulders.

"Holy crap, Emma. Are you really?"

"I don't know. I like him. And I know he likes me."

"Are you in *love*?" She stretches the word in a sing-song and I know she's joking, but I blush anyways, remembering Carter's confession.

"What the? Really? You're seriously in love with him?"

"No," I say, but it doesn't feel right. I don't think I'm in love but quelling it so decisively doesn't feel right either. "But it's a possibility. He says he knows me and that I know him. I mean, I know stuff about him. But the way he talks to me, the way he looks at me. I honestly think he really does know me. It's weird."

"Weird good or weird bad?"

A buzzer sounds in the gym, and all the players start walking off the court. I watch as Carter scans the crowd and his eyes find mine. He unleashes that smile that warms me to the core.

"Weird good," I answer, keeping my eyes on locked on him.

She leans over and hugs me. "That's awesome. Come on, I have to use the bathroom. Keep looking for Red Headband though. He's not off the hook yet."

I let out a laugh and this time I don't get the angst I've had all day. If I see him, then I see him. If I don't, then I don't. I just want to see Carter again.

Chapter 37

Carter

I grab my phone and the red headband from my locker and shoot Emma a text.

BigBaller27: Running late. I just got to the gym. If you want to meet me, feel free to find me

I seriously hope once she finds out the truth she doesn't scream at me and slap me in the face. In all honesty, I probably deserve it. Maybe I should've just told her it was me back when I met her at the oak tree, but she was so furious. And then she told me off.

When I told Coach I needed to put together a half-time performance, he wouldn't hear of it. The team we're playing isn't in the playoffs either, but they're at the bottom of the standings. Even so, he only agreed to it if we held a twenty-point lead by half-time. I worked my ass off during the first half and thankfully, by the time the buzzer rings for half-time, we're up by twenty-three.

"All right, bro." Matt looks over at me. "You sure about this?"

Putting the phone back in my locker, I put the red head-band on. It looks ridiculous, but hey, the things we do for love, right?

I told Matt the plan and got him to help after history class. I'm glad he's my best friend and comfortable in front of crowds since he's going to be on the microphone in front of everyone.

I nod, giving him a confident stare. "Let's do it."

Emma

As we make our way to the bathroom, I get a text from Baller. I deleted our conversation and his number, so it doesn't show his name, but I know it's him from what he writes.

"Jen." I grab her arm.

She turns around and looks at the phone. "Oh, forget the bathroom. Let's find this asshole."

I want to say no. I want to tell her to forget about it. But now that he's texted again, I want to know who he is too. Deleting the text as we walk back, I scan the crowd but don't see anyone.

"Hey." Jen pulls my arm. I spin around, thinking she sees him. "Isn't that Empire of the Sun."

I give her a confused look and then listen. I always play them in my room or her car, so she's heard most of their songs. The moment I hear it, I know it's them. It's my favorite song, *DNA*.

Jen and I give each other confused looks. They played

snippets of music during the game, but all of it was stuff to get the crowd riled up. This is the actual song.

"Ladies and Gentlemen," someone says through the PA system. "We've got a special halftime show for you right now."

I look over at the announcers' table and see Matt. One of the teachers who was making announcements during the game seems annoyed, staring up at Matt with the microphone.

"Most of you guys know we lost a game last week, so we didn't make the playoffs. But tonight's game is a big one. Well, for one player at least." The music is playing along as Matt looks over at me and winks. *What the?*

"We've got a special performance lined up by a *big baller*." I gasp at his words. "He's our starting shooting guard. He's our captain, and he's number twenty-seven. Carter Dixon!"

If my eyes were any wider, they might fall out of my head. I raise my hand to my mouth, unsure I'm even awake.

"No way." Jen gasps.

Carter runs out, bouncing a basketball, now wearing a red headband. I didn't pay attention to his jersey before, but as I watch him now, there it is. Twenty-seven.

"He's quite a *big baller*, isn't he folks?" Matt says to the crowd, again emphasizing the words I know.

Carter finds me and smiles. After a flurry of moves that look extremely hard to do, Matt runs over and brings along with him a rack of basketballs. Unlike the game ball, these are all white and have little red hearts painted on them. I'm still trying to digest everything, as Carter begins shooting.

Carter is BigBaller27? What? How is that even possible? But it is possible. In fact, it's the truth. I'm going through my memories as I watch him shoot. His words that he knows me. That I know him better than I think I do.

Other memories flood through me. Him listening to Empire under the oak tree that day. The nervous habit of rubbing the back of his neck when he'd admit something. Something that I probably should've pieced together. The small things, like bringing me a Pepsi. The big things, like talking about his grandmother passing away or why his parents got divorced.

Then the main memory: Baller didn't stand me up. He was there. Carter knew exactly who I was, but he showed up anyways. He took a chance, and I threw it in his face. Of course, he wouldn't have told me the truth after that. In all the time I've known him, the little attention I showed him was cold and harsh. I thought he was a player who just hooked up with girls.

While everything else runs through my head, Carter grabs the last ball as the song is coming to an end. He pulls off the red headband, and as he walks closer, I see the apprehension on his face.

"I know it's corny." He holds the painted ball out to me with a nervous grin. "Full disclosure, I got the pun from a Valentine's Day card Matt's little brother had."

I look at the painted basketball and see words between the red hearts. *I'm head over hoops for you.* I want to smile, but the shock hasn't worn off. I'm faintly aware that some of the crowd is watching us, but others have started to go about their business. I look back up at him, unsure what to say.

"I'm sorry. I wanted to tell you before, but I just never knew how. And I knew you hated me—"

"I didn't hate you."

"Okay, strongly disliked." He laughs, nervously. "You heard all the rumors. And it's what I let people believe.

Emma, I really do—" He stops and bites his bottoms lip. "Well, I won't say it, because I know what you said before. But now you know. Now you know why I say I know you. Because I do. And you know me too. The real me."

I quickly glance at Jen, standing there dumbstruck, before I meet Carter's eyes again. I know he's telling the truth. More stuff clicks into place. How Baller said he loved basketball, then I remember the memories he told me about going to games with his mom. It was Carter all along.

"Say it."

He gives me an unsure look. "Say what?"

"Say what you told me at lunch." I smile, and it inspires one of his own.

"I love—"

I don't let him finish. My lips crash into his, he drops the ball, wrapping his arms around me. There's noise around us, and I think I hear Jen squealing in excitement, but I'm not sure. I'm not sure about anything around me, only what's going on within me. My hands run through Carter's hair, as he pulls me in tighter. I finally break my lips away from his, looking up into his eyes. He has a little of my lip gloss smeared on him, so I reach up, brushing my thumb over his swollen lips.

"I love you, too."

"You're not mad at me?" he asks with an unsure smile.

"I mean, you could've acted a little more jealous earlier today."

"Don't worry." He laughs. "If you ever tell me that again, I'll handcuff myself to you."

"Oh, kinky," Jen blurts out, nearly deflating the moment we're having.

"I thought you had to go to the bathroom?" I growl at her but keep my eyes on Carter.

"I went already. All this excitement made me pee my pants."

I shake my head at my best friend, just as Carter kisses me again.

"Sorry, bro." Matt walks up behind him. "Coach wants us back in before the half starts."

"I know," Carter grunts, but keeps a hold of me. "Text me after? Since, you know, you already have my number."

"I deleted it," I respond, blushing.

"I'll take that as a good sign that you really do love me."

"My word isn't good enough?"

"Maybe." He grins as I raise an eyebrow. "If you say it again."

"I love you."

"I love you, too."

"Oh, my God!" Jen yells. "You guys can totally send pics now. Let the sexting begin!"

"Jen!" I yell at her, my cheeks blushing, as I watch her walk away towards the restroom.

"I like your best friend." Carter smirks.

"Yeah, you want to trade?"

"I heard that!"

EPILOGUE

Matt

It's been a month since Carter went all *Juno* and confessed his love for Emma, dropping three-pointers in a red headband, outing himself as BigBaller27. I'm happy for him. For them both.

I nudge his shoulder, as I make my way to the lunch table and he scoots over for me. It's been a little weird basically changing friends. Jeremy is such an ass that I don't mind not sitting with him. But I didn't know Lucas has a huge crush on Jen. He doesn't eat lunch with us because he doesn't want to look stupid in front of her. At least, that's what he says. Which I find odd because Lucas has always been a smooth talker. Calm and confident. I think the real reason is that Jen's made it obvious she wants to go out with Franco.

I guess they have two other friends, Micah and Lana, but Emma said they broke up. I know I'm still the new guy, so I don't get the details. I've crossed paths with him a couple of times, but every time I show up at the table for lunch, Micah conveniently takes off. Whatever.

Spring break is coming up, and I'm excited to be heading to New York. My little brother and I are visiting my mom for the week and attending a comic book convention. I've been hiding my excitement though because not even Carter knows I'm a closet nerd. Actually, a HUGE closet nerd. I love to cosplay at conventions. And I don't just go out and buy the costumes; I make them from scratch. I always make sure I have a mask, so that if anyone from school is there, they won't recognize me. But being in New York, I can let my guard down. It's going to be awesome.

"So, come on." Carter nudges Emma's shoulder. "You've been keeping us dangling here."

"Emma, this is ridiculous," Jen says. "We're all here now, and you wanted to tell us at the same time. Just spit it out."

"But Micah isn't here."

"He's been spotty for the last couple weeks."

"I'm getting a little worried about him."

"Don't be." Jen waves her hand. "He's fine. I can't believe he broke up with Lana, but I see him in psychology. He's okay."

"Emma," Carter groans.

"Okay, okay. So ..." Emma reaches around into her backpack and pulls out a folded letter. The smile that spreads across her face is adorable. No wonder Carter fell so hard. "I got the scholarship!" she cries out.

"Ohmygod!" Jen shouts.

"Congrats, Emma," I offer.

"See." Carter wraps an arm around her. "I told you you were gonna get it." He leans over and kisses her.

"There were a lot of great artists who submitted their work."

"Yeah, but your work is awesome."

"Hey, I'm gonna grab a drink. You guys want anything?" I get up from the table.

"Pepsi." Carter and Emma say at the same time, then smile at each other.

I'm happy for them, I really am. But that cutesy, say it at the same time thing? I do everything can to not roll my eyes.

After I pay for the sodas from the snack stand, I start to head back when I see the screen of a laptop open. It's on a YouTube channel about comic books, anime, and all things nerd. Everything I love.

"He's so hot." One of the girls says, leaning over her friend.

It's a channel I've seen before. The host is some college guy who calls himself Geek Dood, which is also the name of his show, and he's going over the latest X-Men release. He looks like one of those hot college guys that girls drool over. These ones obviously are. Except one, and that's when I notice who they are.

Izzy Jacobs, and her two friends.

"Yeah, he's cute," Izzy says, still staring at the screen. "But how does this guy have so many more subscribers than my page? Does sex sell that much?"

"Yes," her friends say in unison. "Izzy, if you wear something a little more revealing, you'd gain a thousand new subscribers."

A grin hits my lips. Isabel Jacobs is hot. She's curvy in all the right places. She's got olive-toned skin, with shoulder-length black hair. And she's known around the school by anyone who likes pop culture stuff because she hosts her own YouTube channel, SoCal Nerd Girl. She covers all the things I love that no one knows about. And it's not just a few hundred followers she has. If I remember right, I think she has over thirty thousand subscribers.

My eyes float back to the screen because I don't think this is an episode I've seen of Geek Dood, and now he's talking about a new cross-over that Marvel Comics is doing with X-Men and the Avengers. I'm so pre-occupied with the video, it's not until I hear a cough that my attention is diverted back to the girls.

"Did you need something, Mr. President?" Izzy looks over at me.

"Oh, no. Sorry." I can feel my face getting red and turn to leave.

She knows who I am, as does most of the school. Not because I'm some popular jock, though I guess you could say I am that, but because I'm class president.

Carter never brings it up, because he knows I only did it to get my dad off my back, but yeah. I've been teasingly called 'Mr. President' more times than I like to remember this year.

But since I'm secretly a fanboy, I'm much more acquainted with Izzy than just knowing her from school. I always watch her YouTube videos, another thing no one knows. And I'll make it out of high school in just a few more months without anyone finding out because like Carter, I do have a rep I like to keep. I'm not as popular as him, but I have my moments. And I like them. I plan on keeping it that way.

FROM THE AUTHOR

Thanks so much for reading Rumor Has It. I really hope you enjoyed Carter and Emma's story, as much as I enjoyed writing it. Please consider leaving a rating and/or review. Ratings and reviews help other readers find the book.

ABOUT THE AUTHOR

RH Tucker lives in Southern California, writes contemporaries and urban fantasy, and drinks too much caffeine. If you'd like to connect on social media, just follow the links below!

For more Info
www.rhtuckerbooks.com

 twitter.com/rhtuckerbooks

 instagram.com/rhtuckerauthor

 facebook.com/rhtuckerbooks

Printed in Great Britain
by Amazon